THE MARK

Published by TROIKA BOOKS

First published 2015

Troika Books

Well House, Green Lane, Ardleigh CO7 7PD, UK

www.troikabooks.com

A CIP catalogue record for this book is available

from the British Library

ISBN 978-1-909991-18-7

1 2 3 4 5 6 7 8 9 10

Printed in Poland

THE MARK

ROSEMARY HAYES

troika books

Chapter 1

Not many loners here. No obvious target.

He walked along the pavement, buildings on either side of him, the shopping mall up ahead.

The Saturday crowds forced him on as they surged forward, the groups of laughing teens indifferent to him, the families with kids – some in buggies, some being dragged along by the hand – all grimly focused on getting to the shops.

He ducked into a doorway, took some deep breaths and closed his eyes, forcing down the rising panic.

The last one.

And after that, what then? Would he finally be free?

When he opened his eyes again, his heart rate had slowed. He looked at the buildings opposite and frowned. There was something familiar about them and he searched for clues – a name above a shop to identify the place, a landmark, anything that could tell him where he was. And then a sickening lurch in his gut as he saw it. The name of the town on a banner strung across the road advertising a forthcoming festival.

God! How could this happen? He was back in the town where it had all kicked off, where everything had gone wrong. Whose crazy idea was that?

He swore under his breath. So *that* was why he'd been given a new name.

There was no way he could use his real name here. Not in this town.

His new name was Jack.

He said it aloud, tried it out, then he pulled his hood further over his head, stuck his hands in his pockets and moved off into the main shopping mall. He looked round carefully and chose a spot out of range of the surveillance cameras, then he shrugged his backpack off his shoulders and sat down against the wall. The pack's material was snagged and stiff with grime, its straps so frayed that only a few threads held them together.

It had been old when he'd left home all that time ago, panicking, shoving things into it, terrified by what he'd done, heaving it onto his back, tiptoeing out the door, closing it softly behind him and then running, his pounding feet loud in the silence of the winter night.

Same backpack, same jeans, same top. Same old.

He blanked his brain and tried to concentrate.

Who would his mark be this time?

They'd told him it would be a girl, he knew that much. He'd recognise her when he saw her; he always did, his senses fine-tuned to pick up the signals.

He scanned the crowds. No one obvious. No scared, lonely youngster to approach. There'd been several since he'd left; vulnerable, easy targets. Thank God he'd never had to get involved. Just the contact, then he'd leave, his job done. He wondered about them sometimes, what was happening to them, but mostly he was glad he didn't know. The last one though, the lad with the violent dad, that had been difficult. Something about that boy had got to him and he'd found it hard to walk away.

Jack coughed, ignoring the pain in his chest. It could be a long time before she showed. He took out his new sketchpad, the one he had nicked earlier, and stroked the top page, leaving a smudge from his fingers on its pristine whiteness, and dug around for the stub of a pencil.

He started drawing.

A few minutes later a figure blocked the light. A security guard, arms folded, stared down at him.

'What you up to, son?'

Jack looked up, startled, tightening his grip on his sketchpad, seeing something familiar in the man – the thick neck, the tall powerful body.

A flashback. He was there again, terrified, running . . .

Stop it!

He held up the sketchpad.

The guard bent down and squinted at it, then he straightened up, giving a quick glance at Jack's frayed sleeves and stained jeans.

'Art student, are you?'

'Yeah.'

Sketchpad. Messed up hair, dirty clothes.

Good call.

The guard nodded and moved away. Jack watched until he was out of sight.

He was hungry and he had no cash but there were some easy pickings here. A group of girls sitting on a bench, their bags on the ground. One of them was holding a phone and the others leaned in towards her, giggling and pointing. Further along, a man was peering into a shop window, both hands cupped over his eyes so he could see better.

There was a wallet in his back pocket. Slowly, Jack got up, grabbed his things and began to walk towards the man.

Bump into him, apologise, ask if he's OK. Usual routine.

Jack would be nowhere to be seen by the time the guy noticed his wallet was gone.

He'd almost reached the man when something

alerted Jack, made him turn quickly and look up, his heart starting to race as his senses heightened, telling him that she was close.

His mark!

He stood very still, the chatter of the shoppers, the movement all around him, the sound of music blaring from a speaker, all fading as he concentrated, making the connection.

Yes, that was her. The tarty, over-made-up girl. Tight short skirt, bleached blond hair, big heels, surrounded by a group of men.

He narrowed his eyes and looked at her more carefully. And then, a jolt of recognition.

God! I know her. I can't do this, I was at school with her – she'll recognise me!

He swallowed and bit his cracked lips.

How the hell is this going to work?

He tried to remember her name and slowly it swam into his consciousness – Rachel? Yes, that was it, Rachel. He frowned. That school had been full of hard kids but she'd stood out as a complete loser, so why was she his mark?

He tried to calm himself, clenching and unclenching his fists, taking more deep breaths. He'd have to go through with it but he'd never had a mark he *knew*! Why were they doing this to him?

There was a swarthy, good-looking dark guy with

her. He had his arm around her waist and there was a crowd of his mates there too, all flattering her and laughing. They'd been buying stuff and were loaded down with bags.

Jack watched, sizing up the situation.

Just then, out of the corner of his eye, he saw the man with the wallet straighten up and go into the shop.

Jack swore under his breath. He'd missed an easy one there.

For the next half hour he did the same thing – sitting and sketching, watching, then making a move towards an open bag or exposed wallet. But he had no luck. Either he couldn't get close enough or the cameras had a good shot of him. And all the time he kept an eye on Rachel and the gang – he knew it was a gang, knew what they were doing – as they wandered in and out of the shops.

People began to stare at him. Notice him. He needed to move away. Then he saw the gang of men again, heading for the exit.

Rachel wasn't with them. She was waving to them as they left.

He had to be sure, so he settled his backpack more comfortably, hitched up his threadbare jeans and followed them out of the mall.

They were just ahead of him now. The good-looking one waved back at Rachel and blew her a kiss. Then she was out of their sight and suddenly the men were laughing and slapping each other on the back.

Snatches of their conversation reached Jack. 'I *lurve* you, baby! You're so beautiful!'

'She's well up for it, the slag. We'll sort her at the party tonight.'

'White trash . . . She'll be so out of it, man.'

Jack stood still, frowning. No doubt about it. She was his mark.

Then he shrugged and reluctantly retraced his steps.

When he got back she was standing alone outside one of the big stores, staring towards the exit. Jack watched her.

After a while, he saw her sit down on the ground, her back against a wall and rummage in the plastic bags. She took out a phone, turning it over and over in her hands. Jack recognised the brand and raised his eyebrows.

Carefully, she put the phone in a handbag so new that it still had the tag attached, and brought out other stuff – a pair of jeans, some tops and shoes. She stared at each purchase in turn, smiling, then carefully returned them to the bags. She hugged herself.

Silly cow, thought Jack.

At last she got up and wandered into the store. Jack followed her at a distance, noticing her hesitancy, sensing that she was out of her comfort zone, unsure now that she was on her own.

For a while she walked around, fingering clothes, then she stopped in menswear and picked out a flashy tie. She took it over to the sales counter.

'How much?' Her voice was harsh, aggressive.

The shop girl looked her up and down, her hostility undisguised. 'The price is on the label,' she said.

Rachel made a show of fingering the tie and looking at the label.

'Too much,' she said, throwing it down on the counter.

She wandered off and stood by a display of fancy scarves, picking at the loose skin at the edges of her nails.

Jack walked quietly towards her. 'Rachel?'

She spun round to face him.

Jack saw himself through her eyes. A scruffy boy standing in front of her, his face half obscured by a hood.

'Rachel?' he said again.

She backed away, scowling. 'How d'you know my name?

He pushed his hood down. He could see that she was having to make an effort to focus on him.

'I heard your friends call you that.'

The lie came easily.

She looked at him for a moment, frowning.

Don't let her recognise me.

Then she shrugged and turned away, but he grabbed her arm.

She tried to pull free. 'Take your hands off me, you dosser!'

Jack held on. He could see one of the shop people look up and stare at them, then start to come towards them. He didn't want a scene.

'Listen,' he said quietly. 'I won't hurt you. My name's Jack.' He was leaning towards her, crowding her. 'I need to tell you something.'

She twisted away from him but his grip on her arm tightened.

'Let go of me, you perve!' She tried to shake free again, her face screwed up and angry as she met his eyes briefly and, again, he saw what he thought was a flash of recognition.

He stayed close, speaking fast. 'I saw you with that gang.'

'What do you mean, *gang?*' Rachel was still trying to pull away, but Jack had her attention now; he relaxed his grip slightly.

'You know what I mean.'

'No, I don't.' She finally shook herself free. 'That's my boyfriend you're talking about. And his friends. They aren't some poxy gang.'

Jack shrugged, still keeping his voice low. 'OK, if

you want to hang out with those guys, it's your business, but don't say I didn't warn you.'

The smallest hesitation.

'Warn me? What are you on about?' Her voice was louder.

'That gang. I know what they do.'

'I'm telling you, they're not a gang. They're my *friends*!' Rachel was shouting now and more people turned to stare at them. Jack started to walk away.

For a moment, Rachel stood still and her hand went to the chain around her neck before she started after him, catching him up at the exit and grabbing his arm. He swung round, automatically raising his fists to defend himself.

She jumped back. 'Hey, watch it!'

Jack's shoulders untensed and he lowered his fists.

She looked at his torn backpack and stained clothes, then back to his face. 'Don't I know you from somewhere? Were you at my school?'

He shook his head but he didn't meet her eyes, didn't answer.

I'm finished if she remembers me.

Rachel looked down at her feet. 'What you said about . . .'

'Yeah, well, whatever. It's your life.'

Jack suddenly convulsed with a fit of coughing. He leaned against the glass of the shop window.

'They've done bad stuff,' he said at last, still gasping for breath.

'What, Adam and his mates? They never.'

Jack straightened up. 'Yeah. Really bad stuff,' he said.

'What are you on about?'

'They groom girls like you.'

As he said it, he knew she wouldn't understand the word. But she latched onto the other words.

'Girls like me? What do you mean, girls like me?'

Jack looked at her, met her eyes, took in the heavy mascara on her eyelashes, the badly applied eye shadow.

'You were in care, weren't you?'

Care. The word hung there between them.

He waited for her to answer but she just scowled at him, defiant.

He went on. 'That's why, Rachel. Because you don't have family. That's why they target you.'

'I don't believe you.' Rachel's voice was less sure.

'I heard them talking,' he said quietly. 'I was behind them when they left the shopping centre. I heard what they said.'

Rachel folded her arms across her chest. 'OK. What did they say, then?'

Jack repeated what he'd heard.

'You're making it up!' But as he watched her face, he could see the uncertainty.

They stared at each other, facing off. Jack pointed to the bags. 'Did they buy you all this?'

Rachel nodded, her face brightening. 'Yeah. Some great gear – clothes and a phone. And other stuff.'

'And give you drugs?'

She hesitated and dropped her gaze.

Jack said nothing.

'What? Why not? What's wrong?' she muttered. 'It's only weed. It makes me feel good.'

Only weed? He didn't believe her. He knew the way these gangs worked.

'Where d'you think their money comes from, Rachel?'

She shrugged. 'Adam's money? I dunno. Anyway, it's none of your business.'

Jack sighed. She really didn't know. He'd have to spell it out. 'He makes his money from dumb girls like you!'

Rachel's head shot up. 'Who you calling dumb, you loser?' She started to move off.

'Didn't you ever think *why* he was giving you all the gear?' he said to her retreating back.

Rachel bit her lip. She stopped and turned round, scowling at him. 'Because he loves me,' she said more quietly. 'He said he loved me and nothing was too good for me.'

'And you believed him?'

'Yeah, course I believed him.'

But the doubt was there in her voice. Again, she fingered the chain at her neck.

Jack watched her face, saw the fleeting frown, the chewing of the lip. He had to say it, had to make her understand.

'Then you're an idiot. He was softening you up, buying you stuff, giving you drugs – just like all the others. *You* were going to make money for them, Rachel. Now it's payback time.'

'What d'you mean?'

Jack raised his eyes to the ceiling. 'You really don't get it, do you?'

She shook her head.

'They're planning to sell you, Rachel.'

'Sell me? What?'

'There are plenty of men who'll pay for sex with a young girl.'

Rachel stared at him. 'Don't say that!' Then her eyes slid away from him. 'He'd never do that. He loves me. He said he loved me,' she repeated.

'Yeah. Well, that's what they do,' he said. Then, seeing her shoulders sag, added, 'I'm sorry.'

She started crying then, her make-up running down her face. Jack stood beside her, awkwardly.

How old was she? He thought back to his time at that school. She'd been a couple of years below him.

He only knew her face because she'd been in so much trouble there. She'd be what – fourteen now?

She dug in her pocket for a tissue, blew her nose and frowned at him. 'Why should I believe you, anyway? What's it to you?'

He shrugged. 'You're right, it's not my problem, Rachel, but you should get the hell out of here. Once they've got you working for them, they won't let you go.'

They stood looking at each other, then she dropped her eyes.

'I can't,' she said at last. 'I'm living at their place. They took me in.'

He shrugged and started to walk away again.

She followed him, the weight of her bags dragging at her arms. 'What shall I do?' she shouted after him.

He heard the panic in her voice and hesitated. He sighed and turned back to her, saw her face streaked with tears and smudged make-up.

'Sorry. I can't help you, Rachel,' he said. He held his hands out to his sides and then let them drop. 'Look at me.'

'First you tell me to get the hell out of here, then you say you can't help me. Effing loser!'

'You could go to the police,' he suggested.

Rachel's eyes flashed with anger. 'The police! You're having a laugh!'

Jack frowned. 'Or the social services.'

She mimicked him. '*Social services.*'

Jack cursed his accent.

'I've had the social on my back all my bleeding life,' she said. 'I don't want nothing more to do with that lot.'

She stood there, scowling at him, then suddenly she dug in her new bag and brought out a purse. She held it out towards him. 'I've got money,' she said. 'I could buy some chips.'

Jack hesitated. He mustn't get involved. But his stomach rumbled. When had he last eaten? He gave a faint smile. None of his other marks had offered to buy him chips.

The last one. Maybe I can . . .

Rachel shook his arm. 'What you doing, talking to yourself? You're mental, you.'

He looked at her blankly. He hadn't realised he'd spoken out loud.

She frowned. 'What are you *on?*'

Then, when he didn't answer, 'You want some chips or what?'

Jack tried to regroup, get his head straight.

'OK. Go on, then,' he said at last.

They found a corner in a crowded McDonalds, slinking in, aware of the eyes of the other customers on them. Rachel gave Jack some money and he ordered shakes, burgers and chips.

As soon as their food arrived Jack fell on it. He was starving!

Rachel ate a few chips and then pushed her plate away.

'Aren't you hungry?'

She shook her head. 'I feel sick.'

'Give it here, then.'

When he'd finished, Jack leaned back in his chair. 'Thanks.'

'OK, now you've stuffed your face, are you going to help me or what?'

Jack put his elbows on the table and stared across at her. 'How much money have you got?'

Rachel frowned. 'What's it to you? I'm not giving you any more.'

'I don't want it, you idiot. Do you have enough to get to another town? Have you got family or friends – somewhere you could go?'

What am I doing? I shouldn't be giving advice. I shouldn't be getting involved. I should be walking away.

She shook her head. 'My family all buggered off, didn't they.'

'Any friends?'

She sniffed. 'Adam's my friend.'

Jack was noisily sucking the last of his milkshake through a straw. 'When are you supposed to see Adam again?'

Rachel frowned. 'He said he'd phone me; he had some stuff to do, then he said he'd come back here and take me to his place to get ready for this party.'

Jack nodded. 'A party,' he said flatly.

Her eyes widened. 'I guess that's when . . . at the party . . . you know, what you heard him saying?' She trailed off.

'And he hasn't phoned yet?'

Rachel dug the phone out of her bag. 'I don't think so.'

'What do you mean, you don't think so?'

She took the phone out of its fancy pink case. 'I only got it today. He told me how to work it but I can't . . . Oh, I dunno. Here, you look.'

'OK. It's switched off, you moron!'

'Who're you calling a moron, you loser?'

Jack didn't answer. He switched the phone on.'OK. There's one voicemail. Do you want to listen?'

Rachel shook her head and Jack could feel the vibration of the table as she jiggled her foot up and down. 'I don't want to hear his voice.'

Jack waited for the voicemail to kick in. As he listened, he stood up sharply, grabbing his backpack from the floor. 'He's on his way. Says he'll meet you at two-thirty under the clock.'

Rachel scraped back her chair and pointed out of the window. 'The clock's just over there.'

Jack looked across at it.

2.25.

They stood looking at each other. 'OK, Rachel,' said Jack. 'It's your call. Are you going to meet him or are you going to make a break for it?'

Her eyes were wide. 'I dunno.' She held on to his arm, tugging at the fabric of his worn hoodie. 'You've got to help me, Jack. I don't know what to do.'

Jack sighed.

This isn't what I do.

'Come on, then.'

They ran out of McDonald's and headed for the road.

'Where are we going?' panted Rachel.

'I dunno. But if you want to leave him we've got to hurry.'

They made an odd pair: Rachel in her short, tight skirt and high heels, and Jack in his dirty, worn out clothes, both weighed down by plastic bags full of Rachel's shopping.

'I can't run in these effing shoes.'

Jack grabbed her hand. 'We'll slow down once we're out of here,' he gasped.

As they passed the clock, there was a shout.

'Rachel! Baby!'

Adam was there. They were all there.

'Adam!' But her voice was a whisper. She hesitated and looked back, unsure.

Jack tugged at her. 'Come *on*!'

She went with him then, but she looked back once more.

'Frigging hell, Jack, they're coming after us.'

'Run faster!'

They shot out of the shopping centre and onto the road.

'Where are we going?' she gasped.

'We'll get on a bus. Try to lose them.'

They looked up and down the road. No buses were coming.

'There's one stopped right up the end there,' said Rachel, pointing further along the street.

'OK. Run for it.'

Jack's chest was tightening but he pushed himself on. At the bus stop there was a queue. They had to stand in line and wait to get on.

'Come on, come on,' muttered Jack, bending over to ease the pain.

Rachel gripped his arm. 'They've seen us.'

Jack looked back down the road. She was right. All of them were there, the whole gang, and they were running up the pavement, shoving people out the way, shouting.

'Quick,' said Jack, pushing Rachel in front of him.

'Hey,' said someone. 'What d'you kids think you're doing? Stop queue-jumping.'

They ignored the shouts. The bus driver hadn't seen. Rachel handed over some money and he looked up, surprised. 'Planning a long trip, love?' he asked, smiling.

When she didn't answer, Jack said, 'To the terminal.'

The bus driver looked at him but said nothing, handed most of the money back and gave them a couple of tickets. Then he revved the engine. 'That's it,' he said. 'No more now. I'm full up.'

The bus doors closed with a hiss, leaving an angry queue of people behind. The engine throbbed and the bus started drawing away from the kerb just as Adam reached it. He banged on the window of the bus and they could see his lips moving, although they couldn't hear him

'You owe me,' he mouthed at Rachel, and he shook his fist.

Jack pulled his hood across to hide his face as he walked down the aisle but he knew Adam was staring at him and he saw the gesture he made.

He was drawing his finger across his neck.

Jack

before

I can still see Mum's face, the way she looked when she told me. I was sprawled on the sofa watching the television when she came into the room and turned it off with the remote.

I'd made a dive at her to snatch it away, but then I'd seen her expression – serious, strained – and slumped back.

'I need to talk to you, love,' she'd said quietly, twisting round to look at me, her brown eyes huge in her pale face, her dark hair falling forward as she leaned in towards me.

I'd looked up at her then and I'd known. Everything had been suddenly still, time suspended. Before she said it, I jumped in.

'It's Dad, isn't it?'

She'd nodded, her eyes not leaving my face.

Don't say it, don't say the word, please don't say it, I'd thought. I'd looked down at the pattern on the carpet, focusing on it, noticing the swirls of pale blue against the darker blue background. Not saying the word might make it go away.

'There's treatment, love,' she'd said at last.

I'd been what – fourteen? – when she told me.

'Will you tell the twins?' I'd muttered.

She'd shaken her head. 'They're too young. It wouldn't be fair.'

It had started a few months earlier. At first Dad had dismissed the back pain, refusing to see a doctor, trying to continue with his life as if nothing was different. But I'd noticed. Dad, always into his sports, slowly giving things up. He'd joked about it. 'Getting too old for all this running about.'

And then the day when I'd walked into the kitchen and seen him, his head slumped on his elbows, his shoulders heaving. I'd never seen Dad cry before. I'd crept out of the room, unable to touch him, say anything. Not knowing words to say, not able to express what I felt but knowing everything would change and refusing to face it. Pretending.

We'd all pretended. To ourselves. To each other.

Chapter 2

They made their way to the back of the bus and squeezed into the last two spaces.

'Great,' said Jack. 'So now he's after me too.'

Rachel sat chewing her nails. 'I shouldn't've left him. Why did you make me?'

Jack raised his eyes to the roof of the bus. The stupid girl wasn't even grateful.

'I didn't make you do anything, Rachel.'

'You so did. You dragged me onto this bleeding bus and you said all that stuff about him, getting me scared. I don't know why I believed you. What if he does love me?'

Jack sighed. 'Fine. Go back to him, then.'

They both stared out of the window as the bus gathered speed, jerking as the driver changed gears, then running smoothly for a while until they reached the next stop. Rachel craned her neck to see who was getting on.

'D'you think they'll catch us up?'

Jack shook his head. 'Not unless they can run faster than the bus.'

'What are we going to do?'

'We? What do you mean, *we*? Just now you wanted to go back to Adam.'

'He's after you, too . . .'

Jack didn't answer. He wasn't going to get sucked into this or hang around any longer than he needed. Just get her away from the gang. Find a safe place for her.

His chest hurt. He shut his eyes, absorbing the pain, but he opened them again as he felt Rachel wriggling beside him. She had picked up one of her plastic bags and was rummaging inside it. At last she drew out a top covered with sequins and held it up to her face.

Jack's temper flared suddenly. What was she like? He snatched up the top and threw it down on the floor. 'All your new gear's not going to help now, is it, you stupid girl?'

'Don't DO that!' shouted Rachel as she bent down and scrabbled on the floor for the top. 'And don't call me stupid,' she continued, when she was upright again.

Rachel continued to stare angrily at him. Jack could see that she was trying to remember.

'I do know you from somewhere,' she muttered.

'No,' he said, turning away to avoid her eyes. 'I've never seen you before.'

Whatever happened, she mustn't recognise him. He waited, bracing himself for more questions, trying to think of plausible answers, but she suddenly lost interest in him. He watched as she put her hands on either side of her head, pressing the palms inwards, her eyes closed, muttering to herself.

'What's the matter?'

She hadn't heard him. He frowned. What was going on in that messed up brain of hers?

Then, after a few minutes she looked at him again with dull eyes.

'What happened to you, Jack?' she said quietly. 'How come you're . . .' She pulled at the fabric of his stained hoodie. 'How come you're like this?'

Jack ran his hand through his hair. 'I don't want to talk about it, OK?'

'OK.'

They sat in silence for a while. Outside the city slipped by. Stop, start, people on, people off.

'What about you?'

Rachel frowned. 'What?'

'What happened to you? Did you ever know your family?'

Her hand went to the chain round her neck. 'No,' she said fiercely. 'Like you said. I've been in care, haven't I? Oh, and some foster homes.'

'Yeah? What were they like, the foster homes?'

She breathed on the glass of the bus window until it misted up and then rubbed her finger across it. Again, Jack noticed her bitten nails and the bits of skin hanging loose at their edge.

God, she's a mess.

'Some of the foster homes weren't bad, I suppose.'

'What about school?' he asked, although he knew the answer, remembered.

She grinned. 'I bunked off school, didn't I? They got sick of me in the end.'

'What, they expelled you?'

'Yeah. Couldn't see the point; I never learned nothing.'

'What so you never –?'

'Stop going on, will you? Look, I said I don't want to talk about it, OK?'

'OK.'

Rachel started chewing her nails again. Suddenly her phone beeped and she jumped. She dug in her handbag and picked it up, holding it as though it was burning her thumb and finger.

Jack leaned over and looked at it. 'Is it him?'

'Must be. He's the only one knows I've got it.'

'What's he say?'

Rachel handed the phone over and Jack read the text out loud.

'Jeez, Rachel, he's one angry man.'

'Yeah.'

They were both silent, then she spoke again. 'I'm shit scared.'

Jack sighed and scratched his neck. 'Isn't there anyone who could help you? Did you have a social worker?'

Rachel exploded with laughter. '*Her*? No way. She hated me. I'd never ask her for no favours.'

Jack looked out of the window. The city was giving way to the suburbs, the houses were further apart now and there were more green spaces.

'When we get to the bus terminal, what do you want to do?'

Rachel shrugged.

'Is there anywhere you want to go?'

Her eyes brightened then. 'London. I've always wanted to go to London.'

Jack smiled. '*London!* What would you do in London?'

'I dunno. Get a job?'

'Oh come on, Rachel, get real!'

She turned to face him. 'Don't keep putting me down,' she shouted. 'Everyone always puts me down. You're no better than me anyway. Look at you, you dosser!'

Several people in front of them turned to stare but when Rachel stuck out her tongue they quickly looked away.

'So,' she went on, lowering her voice, 'you got some

grand plan, then? What are you going to do with your life – or are you going to keep sloping round the shops nicking stuff?'

'Who said I nicked stuff?'

Rachel shrugged her shoulders. 'You saying you don't?'

'No'

She grinned. 'See?'

Did everyone see him like that? A no-hoper, a thief? He looked down at his feet. His trainers were almost worn through, his clothes were rags and he didn't smell great. So why should he think he was any better than her? He was as much of an outcast as she was – out of the system, drifting.

That's how she'd see him, anyway.

'How much money have you got?'

She handed over the purse. 'Don't you go nicking it.'

He allowed himself a smile as he opened up the purse and counted the notes and the coins.

'There's forty quid and a bit of change, Rachel. Won't go far in London.'

She took it back and put it in her bag. 'Why don't you come with me, then? Help me and that?'

'To London? Nah. I'm no good to you, Rachel, here or in London or anywhere else.'

'No, you ain't much bleeding good, but you're clever.'

'If I was clever I wouldn't be having to nick stuff.'

'No, I mean clever about reading and that.'

He looked at her. It didn't shock him. He'd suspected it all along.

'You can't read, can you?'

She looked at him defiantly. 'Yes I can.' He continued to look at her. 'A bit,' she added.

Oh God, she'll have no chance in London. She'll end up on the streets.

Two hours later the bus slowed down for the final time. 'Watercross Grove. This bus terminates here.'

Jack and Rachel got stiffly out of their seats, gathered the bags together and shuffled down the aisle with everyone else. As they alighted, Rachel looked round nervously.

'D'you think Adam knows we're here?' she asked.

Jack shrugged. 'We could have got off anywhere along the route.'

'Yeah. But he could have gone back and got his car and followed us.'

'Stop being so paranoid.'

'Eh?'

'Never mind.' Jack shouldered his backpack. 'OK, so what do you want to do?'

'Go to London?'

'Oh for God's sake, Rachel. If you really want to go to London you'll have to go back into town to the train station or the coach station. We can't go to London from here.'

She looked around her, at the small terminus building and, beyond that the fields and hedges. Unfamiliar, threatening.

Rachel frowned. 'You got a better idea?'

'OK,' said Jack. 'I'll see if I can find out about coaches to London.'

He went inside the building to ask. Rachel stood a little way off, surrounded by her bags, jiggling from one foot to the other.

After a few minutes he rejoined her. 'There's a coach that goes to London,' he said. 'But it's a long way and the ticket costs a fortune.'

'OK. When does it leave?'

'Tomorrow morning. And like I said, you'd have to go back into town to get it. And the last bus back into town has just left.'

'Crap. We can't stay here all night. Hey, where's the toilet?'

'There's one inside the terminal. Look. Over there.'

Rachel tottered off, taking her bags with her.

Jack leaned up against the wall, watching people coming and going. What the hell was he doing with this dumb girl?

He should make a break for it now. Disappear from her life and leave her to sort herself out.

And yet . . .

He kicked out at a stone on the road, sending it skittering into the verge.

After a while, Rachel reappeared. She'd washed her face and reapplied a ton of make-up – and put on some of her new clothes. Jack raised an eyebrow.

'Ready to hit the high life?'

She did a twirl. 'What do you think?'

'Yeah. Great,' he mumbled, taking in the sparkling top and tight jeans.

'Adam says I'm pretty.'

'I'm not Adam.'

She smoothed down her jeans. 'Too right. You're not one to say something nice to a girl,' she muttered, patting her bleached hair. 'So, what's the plan, then?'

Jack put his hands in his pockets. 'Up to you, Rachel. You go off to London if that's what you want, but I'm not coming with you.'

Again she started chewing at her bitten-down thumbnail. 'I'd be scared on my own.'

He felt the anger building up again. 'Look, it's not my damned business. It's your problem. You got yourself into this mess.'

She turned on him. 'No I didn't. You made me come with you. You can help me.'

'Made you! I didn't *make* you do anything.'

He turned to go, walking away from the terminal, but she ran after him.

'Don't leave me here, Jack.' She grabbed hold of his arm. 'Please!'

He shook her off. 'Let go of me, will you?'

'Just for a few days. Just till I can think what to do. Please!'

He rounded on her. 'No!'

She started crying but he went on walking. Surely he could leave her now he'd got her away from that creep?

He heard the sound of her heels clip-clipping along the tarmac behind him, then suddenly she let out a shriek.

'Jack, it's them!'

He wheeled round and followed the direction of her pointing finger. 'That car coming up the road,' she yelled. 'It's Adam.'

He narrowed his eyes to look at it. 'Are you just saying that?'

'For God's sake, Jack. I know what his effing car looks like!'

For a moment he hesitated while Rachel continued to rant.

'What are we going to DO? Where can we go? He'll murder me.'

When Jack didn't reply, she turned away and

started to run. He glanced again in the direction of the car, then he ran after her, caught her up, grabbed some of the plastic bags, towed her by the hand as she stumbled in her fancy shoes, and led her down an alley at the side of the terminal. At the end of the alley they stopped, leaning over, gasping for breath.

'What shall we do?' she panted. 'We can't stay here, he'll search the place.'

Jack pointed to some rubbish bins at the end of the alley. 'For a start we can dump the bags. We can't run with them. We can come back for them later.'

They stuffed the plastic bags behind the bins and Rachel crouched down beside them, sobbing. Jack looked at her as he fought to get his breath back. She was curled up in a foetal position, trying to make herself as small as possible, as if she could make herself invisible, impossible for Adam to see.

A terrified little animal cowering from a predator.

Jack crept up to the top of the alley and peered out. She was right, it was Adam. He and three of his gang were getting out of the car and walking into the terminal. Even from a distance, he could see they were spoiling for a fight, see the swagger in their walk. For a moment he was right back in the school yard.

Tomcats.

He went back to Rachel. She was trembling and she didn't look up until he shook her.

'Quick. While they're inside the terminal we'll run for it. There are some buildings just down the road.'

She raised her head then and held it between her hands, rocking it to and fro. She looked at him as if she'd not understood what he'd said.

'Rachel!' He tugged at her hand and she rose unsteadily to her feet. 'Come on! Run!'

They shot out of the alley and headed down the road.

'My shoes,' gasped Rachel.

'Take them off, you idiot.'

She bent down and yanked the shoes from her feet, then, holding them in one hand, she sprinted after Jack. 'Ow, ow, ow!' she squeaked as her bare feet were pierced by stones.

They made it to the buildings. One of them was a boarded-up warehouse of some sort and there was a path between it and another building. Jack and Rachel managed to reach the path just in time, before Adam and the others emerged from the terminal.

'He didn't see us, did he?'

Jack couldn't speak. He was panting too much, the pain in his chest stabbing at him again. He leaned against the wall and slid down to rest on his haunches.

'Did he see us?' she repeated.

He shrugged.

Rachel came and huddled beside him and put her shoes on again.

Gradually the pain in Jack's chest dulled and they sat together for a while. Once or twice they looked back up to the terminal car park. Adam's car was still there.

'Why's he staying there?'

Jack shrugged. 'He's probably guessed you're still around here.'

'But we could have got off anywhere, like you said. Or we could have got the bus back into town.'

'He's not stupid. He'll have asked people if they've seen us.'

Pretty easy to spot, the two of us.

'Well, he won't wait long, will he?' said Rachel. 'He's got his party later.'

Jack shook his head. 'You're more important to him than any stupid party,' he said, grimly. 'There won't be any party without you. He needs you there for his punters, the sick bastard.'

Rachel shivered. 'What shall we do, then?'

'Wait till he goes,' said Jack.

The minutes went by as they crouched there in silence.

'I'm hungry,' said Rachel.

'Should have eaten more chips, then,' replied Jack. He stood up and stretched, crept to the edge of the building again and then darted quickly back.

'They've found your gear.'

Her hand flew to her mouth. 'You sure?'

'Well, they were stuffing a whole lot of plastic bags into the car,' he said.

'So he knows we've been here?'

'I guess so.'

'Oh God, what if he –?'

Jack eased along the wall and very carefully looked out again, then he jumped back.

'They're coming this way!'

'Shit!'

Jack looked down the path. It veered off to the right and there was a fence at the bottom surrounding a field, and beyond that a small group of trees. He ran down to the fence. Rachel caught him up. She looked behind her, whimpering.

'They're going to find us.'

Jack nodded. He pointed at the fence. 'We'll have to climb through there and leg it across the fields to those woods. If he finds us, it won't be pretty. He's one angry man and I'm in no shape to fight him.'

Him against a gang. Just as it had been when he'd tried to defend himself in the school toilets.

She nodded, took her shoes off again and followed him, bending down to squeeze through the barbed-wire fence and snagging her new top. 'Ow!'

Jack freed her and they started running across the

field. They were very exposed. Adam was sure to look down the path beside the boarded-up building but with any luck he wouldn't explore further, wouldn't bother walking the length of the path. If he did, he'd see them as they ran across the field, tripping and staggering in their hurry.

Rachel was crying again. She had fallen several times and the last time she'd hurt her ankle. Jack stopped for her to catch up, his chest heaving and the sweat pouring down his face.

He held out his hand and she grabbed onto it. 'Nearly there,' he panted.

The last few metres were slow going. She was hobbling with pain and he was too breathless to run any further. As they reached the woods and squeezed under the fence again, they looked back.

'I can't see them,' said Rachel.

'Good. Come on, let's head into the trees.'

They didn't stop until they were deep into the wood, crashing through undergrowth, snapping twigs underfoot, blood pounding in their ears. At last Rachel sank down on the ground, her back against a tree.

'I can't go no further.'

Jack stood beside her and put his hands on his knees, taking great rattling breaths.

'How long do you reckon they'll go on looking for us?' she asked.

He shook his head, still too puffed out to speak.

Rachel looked at her filthy white jeans and bloodied feet. 'My new jeans,' she wailed. 'They're ruined. And look at my feet. They're all bleeding and sore, Jack, and they effing hurt.'

Jack gave a faint smile. 'Not dressed for the country, are you?'

She shook her head.

Jack eased his backpack off his shoulders and squatted down beside her.

'Ever slept rough, Rachel?'

She hesitated, then nodded. 'Yeah. A few times. But not in the country. It's spooky here and there's animals and stuff. It's well creepy.'

'This isn't the real country. It's just the suburbs.'

'How d'you know? Have you lived in the country, then?'

He nodded. 'Yeah.'

She looked at him. 'You're a funny sod, aren't you, with your posh voice and all? What happened to you, Jack? How come you're like this?'

He brushed his matted curls out of his eyes. 'Long story,' he said shortly.

'I'm not going anywhere.'

'And I'm not talking about it.'

She picked up a leaf from the ground and examined it. 'OK, have it your own way.'

They sat there for a while, on a moss-covered tree trunk in the middle of the wood, as the sun slipped further towards the horizon.

Rachel was shivering. 'I'm bloody freezing. We can't spend the night here.'

Jack stood up stiffly. 'You're right. We'll have to find some shelter before dark. Come on. We'll go out the other side of the wood. There'll be houses nearby. We'll see if we can find a shed or something.'

Rachel staggered to her feet. 'I can't walk far, Jack. My feet are knackered.'

'You'll have to. I can't carry you, can I?

When they emerged from the other side of the woods, they saw rows of houses backing onto the field. As she hobbled over the uneven grass, still barefoot, Rachel kept looking round. Every time there was a noise – a dog barking or a car passing down the road in front of the houses – she jerked to a halt.

'Stop being so jumpy. Come on,' said Jack. 'We want to get across this field before dark.'

'I know he's still about,' said Rachel. 'I can feel him.'

'Shut up.'

They struggled through the far fence and into someone's back garden. A big house with welcoming lights at the windows. The curtains weren't drawn and they could see the flicker of a television screen in one of the rooms. Rachel peered towards the window.

'They're well posh, these houses. Wonder what they're watching?'

'Not the stuff you'd watch,' muttered Jack.

'I heard that. What d'you mean?'

'For God's sake!'

There was a garden shed and Jack tried the door. 'Damn. It's locked.'

'I can't go no further, Jack. Honest, my feet are really bad.'

In the fading light, Jack looked across at her. She was a wretched sight now, her clothes covered in mud and grass stains, her feet bloodied. Her bag was still slung over her shoulder and she held her shoes tightly in her hands, hugging them to her.

He stood uncertainly in the garden. What the hell was he supposed to do, lumbered with this brainless girl who couldn't walk?

Suddenly Rachel stiffened.

'What is it?' But then he heard it too. A door opening and a sudden pool of light around it, a woman's voice saying something, then laughing as a dog came bounding out into the near darkness and headed straight for them.

They flattened themselves against a hedge.

'Shit,' whispered Rachel, squeezing herself close against Jack.

The dog could smell their presence and he came

closer, barking furiously. Rachel dug her fingers into Jack's waist and buried her head in his back, but Jack could see the dog's wagging tail and he shook Rachel off and walked forward, calling softly. When he reached the dog, he leaned towards it and stroked its head.

'Hey, boy,' he whispered. 'It's OK. We won't hurt you.'

The dog stopped barking and licked his hand.

'Slowly, now,' whispered Jack, turning to Rachel. 'Walk away slowly. We'll go round the side of the house and get onto the road.'

The dog followed them, whining softly as they made their way to a gate at the side of the house.

'OK, boy,' whispered Jack. 'You stay here.' Then he opened the gate and closed it behind them gently when they were both through. Rachel hobbled after him and they crept over the front garden, through another gate and onto the road.

Rachel

before

I don't really remember her. I was only little. Just flashes sometimes – sort of vision things – of someone cuddling me. And crying. And sometimes singing to me. I think it's her song I hear in my head but I don't really know. Maybe it's just another bit of rubbish muddled up there with all the rest of the stuff I don't understand – the voices telling me things, making me do stuff. Usually it's bad stuff but sometimes . . . well, sometimes I think she's there too.

They told me about her. Horrible words – 'abandoned', 'couldn't cope', 'didn't want you'. I never believed them, though. I believe in her song and I hang on to that. That and the necklace she left for me. And the memory of the cuddling, but it's such a faint memory now, so distant that I have to think really hard so it doesn't slip away for ever.

Chapter 3

A wide pavement ran along the side of the road. 'That's better,' said Rachel. 'It doesn't hurt my feet so much.'

Jack didn't answer. He knew Rachel couldn't walk far. Knew they'd have to find somewhere to spend the night – and quickly. They were exposed now, even though it was nearly dark, walking along this pavement; Adam might drive past at any moment.

There was something familiar about this place. Had he been here once, in his other life, with his mum? He had a vague memory that she'd had a friend who had lived round here – a friend who used to give them fresh vegetables.

His mum. Even now, when he thought of her he found it hard to fight back the tears. He wanted to remember her how she used to be. Small and pretty, dark hair, dark eyes; always alive, laughing, teasing them, filling the house with her warmth. He could picture her, bringing great bunches of wild flowers into the house, crushed against her paint-spattered artist's smock, and arranging them in those pottery vases she loved. He wanted to remember her like that, not frightened and cowed, the light in her eyes dulled.

It came back to him then. A word drifted into his brain.

Allotments.

'What?'

Jack started. He'd done it again. Spoken aloud.

'There might be allotments round here,' he said.

'What's that, then?' asked Rachel.

'Allotments? Where people grow veggies and stuff.'

She shrugged into the darkness. 'Why'd they want to do that?'

He didn't bother answering.

A little later, she stopped and sat down on the road. 'I can't go any further. My feet . . .'

'They can't be far away. Round the next corner.'

What if they aren't there? What if I'm wrong?

Rachel didn't move. Jack bent down and tugged at her hand.

'Please, Rachel.'

'I'm not going anywhere.'

'There'll be sheds.'

'How d'you know? You got second sight or something?'

'Trust me.'

'Huh!' she said, but she got slowly to her feet.

He was still holding her hand as she limped forward, but she pulled it away roughly.

They made slow progress and Jack held his breath as they turned the corner. Would they be there?

Yes! He punched the air.

He could just make out the shapes of some sheds.

'See? I was right!'

'No, I can't see a bleeding thing. It's dark.'

'Well, they're there.'

Jack put his backpack on the ground and scrabbled inside. He brought out a torch and switched it on, sweeping it round in an arc. Its beam was very dim but occasionally it picked out a wigwam of sticks with beans beginning to climb up them and neat rows of other vegetables, unidentifiable in the near darkness.

On some of the allotments there were small sheds.

Rachel peered. 'How did you *know?*'

He shrugged into the darkness. 'Just a guess,' he muttered.

'Eh?'

'Forget it.' He wasn't going to explain, wasn't going to let her in on any part of his past life.

They blundered over the allotments, going from one shed to the next, and at last they found one with a flimsy padlock. They uprooted a metal stake from one of the rows of plants and with it they managed to prise the lock off the door. The sound of splintering wood was scarily loud in the dark and they stood very still for a few moments in case anyone had heard them. Then they pushed the door open and crept inside.

'Ow!' said Rachel, stubbing her toe.

'Shh! Be quiet, for God's sake.'

Jack shone his torch round the shed. 'This'll do. Look, there's a heap of sacks over there – and a big bag of something we can use as a pillow.'

Rachel didn't say anything.

'Well, it's better than being out in the open,' said Jack.'Come on, then. Help me shift this stuff.'

'Why should I?'

Jack bit back an angry answer and started clearing a space to sleep. Rachel stood and watched but when Jack started to cough, she sighed.

'S'pose I'll have to help now or you'll have one of your bleeding coughing fits.'

They moved all the empty sacks into a corner and huddled together under them, using a bag of fertiliser as a pillow.

Rachel dug in her bag and Jack watched her as she rolled a spliff, the acrid smell wafting into his face as she dragged on it. She waved it in front of him.

'Want a go?'

He shook his head. 'Doesn't do it for me.'

It never had.

'Go on. It's my last one.'

He shook his head.

'You're so straight, Jack. You're like a bloody teacher.'

He put his hands behind his head and watched in silence as she smoked, the uneven glow from the burning paper showing up in the gloom of the shed.

She took a final drag, stubbed it out on the floor, and snuggled down by his side. After a while she put her arms round his waist.

He prised them off him. 'What are you doing?'

She giggled. 'I'm feeling horny, Jack.' Her words were slurred.

Jack rolled away from her and went and stood against the door of the shed.

Rachel sat up. 'Don't you fancy me? Adam fancied me. He said I was hot.'

'Go back to him, then,' said Jack.

'What's the matter with you?'

Jack couldn't see her face in the darkness.

'Is that what you think, Rachel? That the only thing a boy wants from you is sex?'

She shrugged, and giggled again.

'I don't want sex from you, Rachel.'

'Why? You gay or something?'

He smiled into the gloom.

She was quiet for a bit. Then she said, 'I've never had a bloke be just a friend.'

He lay down again then and she didn't try to touch him this time, but his thoughts kept him awake; she had stirred up feelings he'd hoped he'd buried along with the rest of his old life. Slowly he began to drift off, only to be woken by Rachel's voice.

'Jack?'

'What?'

'You going to check the phone?'

'No. Go to sleep. We'll look in the morning. Night.'

'Night, then.'

Before long Rachel was stretched out, breathing heavily, but Jack was wakeful, fretting. For a while, the pain in his chest was bad, but then it gradually receded and he began to feel stronger. He had found them a good place.

A few hours later, Jack suddenly jerked awake. He crawled out from under the sacks and sat up. Something had woken him; he'd been used to the feeling when he'd been on the run, that sense of ever-present danger, the threat from every little noise. He felt in his backpack for his torch and swept the beam round the shed. It was so weak he could only make out the shapes, the outlines, but then the light picked out a pair of shiny eyes. He relaxed. Only a mouse!

Good thing Rachel didn't see it.

He didn't lie down but stretched over Rachel's sleeping form to pick up her handbag. He took out the phone and then, getting to his feet as quietly as he could, he went outside the shed and switched it on.

Five texts. Each saying the same thing, each one more angry than the last.

You can't hide from me, you bitch. You owe me – remember.

And much worse.

Jack deleted them all and then switched off the phone.

It was a still night and the sky was blazing with stars. There was a thin haze of pollution but it was much clearer here than in the city. He looked up and took a long, deep breath. When he'd lived in the city he'd missed the countryside where the night skies were really clear. He stood staring at the stars for a while; his dad had known the names of the constellations and tried to teach him, but he'd never remembered.

Dad.

Dad, Mum, the twins. That safe, secure life seemed an age ago. How casually he'd accepted it as his right, never dreaming it would change – how he would change, turn into a thief, a dosser, a criminal.

And a boy with a burden of overwhelming guilt.

Don't. Don't go there.

After a while he sighed and turned back to go inside the shed.

* * *

It was late when they woke up, the sun blazing in through the tiny grime-covered window in one side of the shed. Rachel shook Jack.

'Hey, wake up. It's late – someone'll find us.'

Instinctively, Jack sat bolt upright, then relaxed as he looked around him and remembered. He checked his watch; he'd been given it for his sixteenth birthday. Only a few months ago. In another life. The only thing of value he'd been able to hang on to.

'Jeez, it's nearly ten o'clock,' he said, jumping to his feet.

Rachel looked down at her feet and Jack followed her gaze.

'They hurt?'

She nodded. Jack helped her up and she winced as she put weight on her bad ankle.

'I need a crap.'

'Go behind the shed, then.'

'What?'

'For God's sake, Rachel. Squat down behind the shed.'

She limped towards the door. 'What do I use for . . . ?'

'Leaves,' he said shortly.

'Eh?'

'Big flat leaves. Ideal.' Being on the run had taught him stuff.

'Leaves! That's gross!'

'Got a better idea?'

She shrugged.

'Careful. Make sure no one's about.'

She giggled. 'No, I don't want no one seeing my bare arse, do I?'

She opened the door a crack and peered out before opening it fully and slipping through.

When she came back, hauling on her jeans, Jack was ready to go.

'Nothing worth nicking, is there?' she said.

Jack shook his head. 'I wouldn't steal from here.'

'Why not?'

He looked her full in the face then, his eyes angry. 'I only steal when I have to.'

'OK. No need to bite my head off.'

They crept out of the shed into a beautiful summer's day. They walked slowly across the allotments, Rachel hobbling, as they made their way onto the road.

Just before they turned the next corner, Jack looked back.

The shed was still there; their retreat, solidly squat. Coming upon it last night had been so lucky, so meant. Although he knew that luck had nothing to do with it, he'd still half expected it to vanish in the light of day.

Rachel was limping badly, biting her lip against the pain. 'It's no good,' she said, and she stopped and sat down at the edge of the road.

Jack glanced about him. A little further on he could see a park. That would have to do. He turned to Rachel and pointed.

'There's a park there with a playground – swings and stuff. I expect there's a toilet too. You stay there and I'll go ahead and see what I can find.'

I'll get her some food and stuff and then surely I can leave her.

'What if Adam –?'

'Go in the toilet. Adam won't look for you there.'

'Huh. You don't know him.' Then she dug in her bag and brought out the phone. Jack watched her carefully.

'There's another text,' she said, handing the phone to Jack. 'What's it say?'

Jack read it. The threats were worse now.

'What's it say?' she repeated.

Jack shrugged. 'Same old stuff. Don't worry. He'll give up. You'll soon be in London. He won't come after you there.'

Rachel snatched back the phone and Jack watched as she frowned at the message and mouthed out the letters. She recognised some of the words – the bad ones.

She looked up at him, her eyes filling with tears. Carefully she dropped the phone back in her bag.

They walked over to the park, Rachel still barefoot, her feet too swollen to fit into her shoes. It was a slow business but at last they were sitting on a bench by the swings. Two mothers with toddlers were there and they gave Jack and Rachel suspicious looks and moved away.

'Give us the phone,' said Jack, holding out his hand. Rachel hesitated. 'It's OK. I only want to look at something.'

She handed it over and Jack started scrolling across. He'd had one of these once, in his other life.

'What you doing?'

Jack flipped expertly through the apps to a map. 'Might as well see what else is around here.'

'Like what?'

He didn't answer but just kept fiddling with the phone.

At last he put it away. 'OK, here's what we do.'

'You got some brilliant plan now?'

He shrugged.

'So?'

'There's a shopping centre not far away. I'll leave you here and see what I can scrounge.'

'Eh?'

Jack sighed. 'You'll need some clean clothes and proper shoes, Rachel. And food.'

'How you going to get that, then? I've not got much money.'

He shook his head. 'I've got ways.' Then he said, 'But I'll need a bit of cash too.'

She didn't take out her purse. Instead she looked at him, frowning.

'You're gonna leave me here and bugger off, aren't you?'

He sighed. 'No. I'll be back soon as I can.'

'You swear it?'

'Swear it.'

She gave him some money and he started towards the road, and then he turned round and came back.

'Can I take the phone?'

He saw her hesitate and knelt down beside her.

'I promise I'll come back, Rachel, with the phone and with some food and clothes.'

If I can.

She nodded and handed over the phone.

Rachel watched him go.

The voices were there again, muttering, jangling somewhere in the back of her head. Sometimes they were clear, telling her to do things, but now the words were all jumbled, getting louder and louder. She put her hands over her ears and rocked her head from side to side. Gradually they became quieter, whispering unintelligible messages, until they died right down and the tune came through.

Always the same tune.

It had been bad before – when she'd run away from

the care home. But now the voices and the tune were with her all the time.

She thought of Tracey, the only friend she'd ever had in that place; they'd been good together, trusted each other with secrets, but Tracey had been sent away and they'd lost touch. Her own fault, she supposed, because Trace had sent her that letter she'd never answered. It hurt when she thought of Tracey, and the voices in her head began again, even louder this time.

Mutter, mutter, mutter, interspersed with the occasional shout.

Rachel rocked her head more violently to try to shake them free, but nothing would shift them. 'Stop it, stop it!' she said, scratching her arms and swaying from side to side.

'Try the song,' she told herself. Sometimes that worked. That tune she'd known for ever in her head; it had been there before the voices came. As long as she could remember. Sometimes, if she sang it, she would feel arms around her, keeping her safe, and someone kissing the top of her head. She started humming, softly at first and then louder and louder until at last the voices were drowned out.

Wearily she raised her head and became aware of the other people in the park.

The smug mums in the playground with their shiny

clean kids were sending her death stares, so she got up and limped into the toilet.

It was two hours before Jack came back. Rachel had given up on him. She was back sitting on the bench again, her face blotched with tears, shivering, cradling her head in her hands and rocking to and fro. When she saw him coming across the park towards her, she jumped up and hobbled over to him, shrieking.

'Where the hell have you been, you bastard?'

And when she reached him she started to bang him on the chest with her fists.

Two women walking their dogs turned to look at her.

'See,' she screamed. 'It's like this all the time. People staring at me. I bet they've sent for the cops.'

Jack was tired. 'For Chrissake, Rachel, calm down, will you? And shut up. Stop yelling at me.'

She started snivelling. 'I thought you'd buggered off and left me,' she said more quietly.

'I *told* you I'd come back, you idiot.'

'Don't call me that!'

Rachel allowed herself to be led back to the bench and Jack opened his bulging backpack. He hauled out some trainers, a pair of jeans and a jacket.

Rachel stared at them. 'What's this?'

'I had to guess the size.'

'I'm not wearing this rubbish!'

Jack took her by the shoulders and shook her. 'Look, you stupid cow, I've brought you some clean stuff you can wear. If you don't like it, then screw you; I'll leave you here and you can take your chance on your own.'

Rachel sniffed and picked up the jeans. 'Where did they come from?'

'From a supermarket.'

'What d'you mean? They're not new.'

He shook his head. 'No, I got lucky. The jeans and jacket were in a bag beside those recycling bins they have.'

'And the shoes?'

'From a charity shop.'

Rachel picked up the shoes and frowned.

Jack dug in his pack again. 'I bought some plasters and a roll of bandage too. For your feet.'

Rachel rubbed her eyes and sniffed. 'Thanks.'

'And I got some food. Out of date stuff, but it should be OK.'

'How did you get that?'

'I know how these places work.'

Rachel looked at him. 'You been living like this for a while, then?'

He was noncommittal. 'Off and on.'

She said nothing but looked down at her bitten nails with the chipped black polish, and turned the pair of trainers over in her lap.

'Go on, then,' he said.

'What?

'Go and sort out your feet and put on your new clothes.'

'Huh! New clothes. As if!'

But she heaved herself off the bench and went back into the toilet. A little while later, she emerged.

'How are the feet?'

'Yeah, they don't hurt so much now. It's just the ankle.'

She'd not used the bandage so Jack took it from her. 'Sit down,' he ordered, and he rolled up her jeans, took off the trainer, then bound her ankle.

'That should give you a bit of support.'

'Right little doctor, aren't you?'

'Stand up, Rachel. See if you can walk better.'

Carefully, she tested her weight on the bad ankle. She sniffed and drew the back of her hand across her nose. 'Yeah, that's better.' She sat down again. 'What are we going to do now?'

Jack brought out the food he'd scrounged. An odd assortment of packages. He had a spoon in his backpack and they dug at the bean salad, buns and chocolate mousse in turns.

Rachel was jiggling her legs and hugging herself. Jack gave her a quick glance.

'What?' she said.

He'd already looked away. 'Nothing,' he muttered.

She moaned about the food but when Jack didn't bother to answer, she ate her share.

After they'd eaten, Jack handed back the phone and Rachel put it in the pocket of her charity-shop jacket without looking at it and seeing he had turned it off.

He didn't tell her about the new threatening messages. He stretched his arms above his head.

Rachel was fiddling with her hair, putting strands of it behind her ear.

'Jack.'

'What?'

'I need a fix.'

He wasn't surprised. He'd seen the signs: the mood swings, the nervous gestures. The spliff was the least of it. That bastard Adam had probably got her onto the hard stuff too.

'I can't get you drugs, Rachel.'

She raised her head. 'I've still got a bit of cash.'

Jack closed his eyes, forcing down his impatience. 'Please, Rachel. I know it's hard. But I can't help you if you do this.'

She raised her hand to bang the side of her head, and as she did so, her sleeve rode up he saw the marks on her arms – deep jagged slashes, some livid scars, some still raw.

Oh God, not that too.

'I need a fix, Jack. It makes me feel good. You don't understand.'

'Yes I do. I've been there,' he muttered.

She stared at him.

He stood up and turned his back on her. It was one of the ways he'd tried to block out the bullying, the situation at home. But it hadn't worked. Nothing had worked.

'Please, Rachel,' he said, still not facing her. 'Please try.'

She started to cry, then, shouting between the sobs.

'I need it, you bastard. I've got to have it. You've got to help me get some, Jack. You're clever, you'll find a way.' She looked round the park. 'I bet there's someone round here who –'

'Stop it!'

He sat down beside her on the bench, feeling her whole body shaking beside his. He saw the beads of sweat on her forehead.

He said nothing as she looked at him. 'Jack, I really need –'

'No. Not that, Rachel. I can't.'

'Bastard,' she muttered, clamping her hands between her knees to stop them shaking.

It was a while before either of them spoke. Jack was the first to break the silence. 'Do you really want to go to London?'

Rachel shrugged. 'Not on my own. Do you want to?'

Jack shook his head, then suddenly began coughing.

'That cough's bleeding horrible.'

Jack ignored her, and when his coughing fit stopped, he continued. 'We can't go anywhere without money.'

The *we* hung in the air between them.

'Well, I'm hanging on to –'

'Not yours, you idiot. I mean we earn it.'

'Earn it. What, work for it? Not nick it? I thought that's what you did, nick stuff.'

He turned and looked at her. 'I told you I only steal when I have to.'

'Oh yeah.'

Again he bit back an angry response and continued. 'There's a fruit farm about twenty miles from here.'

'So?'

'They want pickers. I saw an ad.'

She burst out laughing. 'They'll never take us on.'

'I rang them,' said Jack. 'They didn't sound too fussed.'

'You already spoken to them?'

He nodded. 'It'll be hard work.'

He didn't understand, himself, why he'd done it. It was a spur of the moment thing. Help her get a bit of money together, make her plans, then – surely – he could go. He'd never stayed so long with a mark.

She frowned and looked down at the ground. 'I don't want to do dirty work like that.'

'Fine! Forget it. You do whatever you want. I'm off out of here.'

He got up from the bench but she grabbed his arm. 'Don't leave me here, Jack.'

He didn't answer and yanked his arm free. Then he picked up his pack and slung it onto his back.

'All right, all right,' she shouted. 'So I'll come to the sodding farm place with you.'

He hesitated. 'You sure?'

She nodded.

'You'll have to watch your mouth.'

She looked up at him. 'Think I can't shut my face when I have to?'

Jack grinned suddenly. 'Don't know. But I don't want you causing me any grief.'

'As if!'

They set off down the road, Rachel constantly looking behind them for signs of Adam.

'What'll we do if he finds us?'

'He'll have given up by now,' said Jack.

Rachel sniffed and wiped her nose on the back of her hand. 'I told you,' she muttered. 'You don't know him.'

They walked slowly, holding out their thumbs whenever a car came down the road but no one stopped to give them a lift. The morning wore on and Rachel's feet started hurting again and Jack's chest was tight so they sat down on the verge and had a drink of water.

Rachel rubbed her feet. 'Where d'you want to go, then, when you've got some money?'

At first, Jack didn't answer.

'Hey, you listening?'

Jack carefully plucked a stalk of grass and chewed it. 'There's somewhere I need to go . . . have to get back to.'

'Yeah? Where's that, then? Is it near London?'

He shook his head.

'Further than London, then?'

God, she was irritating!

'Yes. Further than London.'

He'd help her get some money together then he'd go.

He stood up and started off down the road without looking back.

'Hey, wait!' Rachel staggered after him and caught hold of his arm.

'Where d'you want to go, then?'

'None of your business.'

They walked on slowly. Jack shut his ears to Rachel's constant moaning but, after about half an hour, her rants at him became too loud to ignore.

'Why did you bring me here?'

'I hate this. I want to go back to town.'

'My legs hurt.'

'I'm hungry.'

'I can't go on any more. I need a fix.'

This last was yelled at him, disturbing a magpie that rose from the hedge, flapping and squawking in alarm.

Jack stopped then and turned round. Rachel was a wretched sight. Crying now, picking at her clothes, scratching her arms and stamping her feet.

'I can't do this!'

'OK, OK,' he said. He pointed to a group of trees a little further on. 'We'll rest up in the shade under those trees.' Then when she didn't respond, he added, 'We've still got some biscuits.'

She was standing in the road, all restless movement. '*Biscuits!*' She spat out the word. 'What use are bloody biscuits?'

He went to her and took her hand. 'Come on. Just to the trees, Rachel.'

She sobbed all the way there but allowed herself to be dragged along. Jack squeezed through the hedge and helped her through after him, then they sat down under the shade of a large beech tree. He handed her a few biscuits and she took them without speaking, sniffing as she ate.

Jack leaned back against the trunk of the tree.

'Look, we can stay here a bit. We can see a long way from here. If a car comes along, I can run out onto the road and try to hitch.'

She was unresponsive, plucking at her sleeve, staring at the ground.

'Once we get to the fruit farm you can earn some money, then you can go to London.'

'Whatever.'

Jack sighed and closed his eyes. Might as well get a bit of rest; he'd hear the sound of an engine if a car came along.

He hadn't meant to go to sleep but the heat had made him drowsy. One moment he was lying on his back, his hands behind his head, looking up at the sky through the canopy of beech leaves, and the next moment he was dreaming. Not a nightmare this time, not one of the horrors that had him jerking awake, shivering, with sweat beaded on his forehead. This time it was a gentle dream. The smell of the leaf mould and the sound of birdsong taking him back to a happier memory. He was coming down the hill after a walk with Dad and they'd seen Mum and the twins at the bottom, running to greet them. Then they'd settled down for a picnic in the sunshine. He was chasing the three-year-old twins until they shrieked and hiccupped, then he flung himself down beside his mum and the twins immediately pounced on him, tickling him until he begged for mercy.

He woke slowly from the dream and looked about him, taking a moment to understand what was happening, where he was. Then he saw Rachel, curled up on the ground beside him, her knees tucked up into her chest, her thumb in her mouth.

He sat there for a while looking at her, innocent in sleep. Then, in the distance, he heard the sound of an engine.

He shook her. 'Get up, Rachel. There's a car coming.'

She looked at him, sleepy, uncomprehending, then slowly she stood up and stretched.

'Come on,' he said. 'We'll miss it if we don't hurry.'

Jack grabbed his backpack and was already pushing through the hedge and onto the road. He saw a red car coming down the road towards him.

Suddenly there was a shout behind him.

'Jack, it's him! It's Adam!'

Jack doubled back through the hedge again, scratching his hands and face in his hurry. He fell onto the ground the other side.

'What?'

'It's him.'

'You sure?'

She nodded, her eyes wide.

They crouched behind the hedge as the car approached.

'It is,' whispered Rachel. 'It's him. God, Jack, what are we going do?'

The car began to slow down.

'Did he see you when you were on the road?' she asked. She had begun to tremble.

'I don't know,' said Jack. 'He could have.'

The car drew up on the other side of the hedge. The doors opened and three men got out.

Rachel felt for Jack's hand. 'Don't let him get me,' she whispered.

There was no time to think. Jack grabbed their things and, pulling Rachel behind him, he plunged into the woods. The noise of their feet crashing through the undergrowth was magnified in their ears, the dry twigs beneath them cracking like gunfire, the birds flying up from the branches of the trees, squawking in alarm. Rachel kept up with him, fear pushing her on. Jack's chest felt as if it would burst but he forced himself to keep running. The trees grew more densely together the further they penetrated the wood and the undergrowth was more hostile, tearing at their legs, scratching their arms.

Behind them they could hear shouts and the sound of more crashing, punctuated with swear words.

Jack stopped suddenly and Rachel cannoned into him.

'What the –?'

Jack was doubled over. 'I can't . . . run . . . any . . . more.'

'We can't stop now – they'll get us.'

Jack raised his head. 'Ever climbed a tree, Rachel?'

'You what?'

He staggered over to the smooth trunk of a beech tree. There were some low-slung branches and, with the last of his energy, he heaved himself up onto the lowest branch and held out his hand to her. 'Quick, before they see us. Hurry!'

'I can't . . .'

'Don't argue, just do it!'

She hesitated, then there were more shouts behind them and she was suddenly galvanised into action. She grasped Jack's hand firmly and then heaved herself up beside him.

'They'll see us!'

Jack didn't answer. He was already climbing higher. He didn't wait for her but just climbed steadily upwards. Jerkily, biting her lip with concentration, her feet slipping and sliding until she could get purchase on a branch, Rachel followed him. There were voices below them now, coming closer all the time. Jack didn't dare look down but just scrambled upwards as fast as he could until he found a branch well hidden from the ground, then he straddled it and leaned down to help Rachel up beside him.

'Christ, Jack –' she began, but he put his finger to his lips.

They sat there as still as they could, panting, struggling to keep quiet.

Seconds later the men were there. Jack had hoped they'd run on past the tree and then give up the chase and go back to the road, but they stopped just below them. From his vantage point he could see them clearly and he knew if they just looked up, they'd spot him and Rachel. His heart was beating so loudly that surely they must hear it. He risked glancing quickly at Rachel and then, as he looked back down at the three men, for the first time he felt some connection with her. She didn't deserve to be used by low life like them.

Adam and his two mates were breathing heavily. One of them leaned against the trunk of the tree, one of them was bent double, his hands on his knees. Only Adam was looking around.

They looked so urban and out of place in this wood. Jack saw Adam pick up one foot and look at the bottom of his designer trainers in disgust, and then carefully pick out some leaves and thorns from his trousers. The guy leaning against the tree spoke to him.

'There's no one in this frigging place, Adam.'

'Someone was here. We heard them, didn't we?'

'Yeah, but it doesn't mean it was her.'

'Bloody bitch!' said Adam. 'She's too dumb to get far. We'll find her.'

'Yeah. Course we will.'

'I've got clients, haven't I? What am I going to say to them? That I've let their little piece of tail run away? How's that going to make me look?'

The third guy straightened up. 'We'll find her. She's got that phone.'

Adam rounded on the guy. *'We'll find her, we'll find her,'* he mimicked. 'You were supposed to be keeping an eye out for her weren't you and you effing let her get away with that dosser.'

'You never said I had to –'

'Aw shut it. You hang on to me like a bleeding leech. You'd be nothing without me.'Adam spat on the ground. 'I'm not spending any longer in this place – it gives me the creeps.' He turned then and stumbled off in the direction of the road but he'd not gone far before he tripped and fell in a patch of nettles. He screamed and yelled, cursing Rachel, his friends, everything, until he ran out of breath.

Jack smiled grimly. Adam just couldn't hack it outside his sordid little world.

Rachel nudged him. Her hand was over her face and she was trying not to laugh out loud as she watched Adam hopping up and down.

They sat on the branch for a long time, well after they had heard the sound of the car's engine roar into life and its throaty noise had disappeared.

At last, warily, they began to climb down the tree.

'I never climbed a tree before,' said Rachel as she scrambled down to the ground. 'I suppose you were climbing them all the time when you lived in the country,' she added, saying *in the country* with a mock posh accent.

Jack ignored her.

But she was right. Back then, before it had all gone wrong, he was always outside, running along the beach, climbing trees, swimming, hill walking with Dad. Rachel would never understand – how could she, brought up on some sink estate probably, and then a care home. She was an urban creature ill at ease away from the city streets. Just like Adam.

He threw his backpack to the ground and then jumped down from the last branch. Rachel was picking leaves and twigs out of her hair.

'I'm scared he'll come back,' she said. She was twitching and her eyes were screwed up.

Jack recognised the signs.

'We'll just have to risk it,' he said shortly. 'We can't stay here.'

They passed the flattened patch of stinging nettles where Adam had fallen. Jack pointed at it and they both giggled, easing the tension for a moment.

'Serve him right, the scumbag,' said Rachel.

When they reached the road, Rachel looked

nervously up and down, unwilling to leave the shelter of the hedge. Jack dragged her onto the road and began to walk purposefully ahead, his thumb stuck out whenever there was the sound of a car coming up behind. Rachel was progressing crablike, twisting back to look behind her all the time and starting at every sound.

A couple of cars slowed down but then the drivers peered at them from the safety of their seats, glanced hurriedly away and speeded up again.

'For God's sake, Rachel, you're acting like a mad woman. No one's going to give us a lift if you prance about like that. Relax!'

'That's easy for you to say,' she muttered.

'He's after me too.'

'Huh! You're no good to him.'

'Why's he want you back so badly, Rachel? Is it just his clients?'

'You mean the men who . . .?' She shuddered. 'Ain't that enough?'

They'd been walking for nearly an hour and Jack was trying to think how else they could put distance between themselves and Adam, and get to the fruit farm. Rachel was moaning and jittery beside him and he'd almost given up hope of a lift when a lorry drew up a little way past them, and the driver put his head out of the cab window.

'Where you going?' he asked.

Jack ran forward. 'To the fruit farm at Oakley. You going that way?'

The driver nodded, then looked down at them more closely, frowning.

He's sorry he stopped. He doesn't like the look of us.

'We're students,' Jack said quickly. 'Art students. We're going fruit picking to earn some money.'

The man said nothing. Jack saw him take his foot off the brake and reach for the gear stick.

He's thought better of it. He's going to drive away.

'Please,' said Jack. 'We need some money.'

Whatever battle the driver was having with himself, he reached a decision.

'OK,' he said, sighing. 'Hop in.'

Jack and Rachel clambered up into the cab as the engine throbbed.

'You looking to work at Oakley, then?' said the driver as he started off again, changing up through the gears.

Jack nodded.

The driver glanced across at him. 'They're a rough old lot there, son.'

Rachel sat further back in her seat. 'What d'you mean?'

He shrugged. 'Odds and sods,' he said. 'People come from all over – Eastern Europe and that.'

'So?'

The driver turned the wheel and swung out into the road. 'Just saying you kids'll need to watch your backs.'

Jack said nothing.

He was used to watching his back.

Jack

before

I keep seeing the coffin. Still. It was such a beautiful day when it should have been wet, gloomy, anything but full of birdsong and that early summer freshness. Mum hadn't let the twins come so we were alone in the front pew at the church. She kept trying to take my hand but I wouldn't let her. If she'd touched me, I knew I'd cry. And I wasn't going to cry.

'Look after your mum.' That was one of the last things Dad said to me when we finally all knew it was going to end. When the treatment wasn't working. When he was wasting away, gaunt and a sickly pale. Nothing of the old Dad left except those piercing blue eyes of his, anxious, boring into me.

I still feel bad that I couldn't touch him, couldn't bear it when he reached out to me. It was a dad I didn't recognise and his diseased body disgusted me.

I couldn't tell him I loved him. And it embarrassed

me when he said that sort of thing to me. I'd look away and mumble something, desperate to escape from the charged atmosphere, uncomfortable, putting all the bad stuff into some compartment of my brain labelled *Don't go there*.

Stupid! Stupid! What would it have cost me to get the words out? He was dying, for God's sake.

And I never kept my promise to him, did I?

I didn't look after her.

Chapter 4

The lorry stopped outside the farm gates and Rachel and Jack clambered down from the cab and stood there. Jack raised his hand and waved as the driver revved the engine and disappeared in a cloud of diesel fumes. Rachel stood beside him, jiggling from one foot to the other.

They trudged up the farm track, Rachel staring around her. Halfway, she stopped.

'There's nothing here,' she said. 'No houses or shops or nothing.'

'It's a farm, Rachel. You know, where they grow things.'

'I know that! Think I'm stupid?'

Jack smiled.

The track was rutted and the verges beside the track were clogged with weeds a metre high, the fence posts on either side were rotting, and the barbed wire sagging. Jack raised his head and looked at the sky. He could see a plane, way up high, leaving a vapour trail against the blue. He stopped and took a deep breath.

'It's good to be right out of the city,' he said.

Rachel scowled. 'I don't like it. It's too quiet.'

At the end of the track there was a big barn, with tiles missing from its roof and slats of black creosoted wood hanging loose at the sides. They could see some people inside and, as they drew nearer, hear voices.

Trestle tables were lined up along one end of the barn and most of the people were crowding around them while some girls behind the tables were weighing trays of fruit and making a note, then handing slips to the pickers.

Just before they went into the barn, Jack put a hand on Rachel's arm.

'They'll ask for a deposit,' he whispered.

'What?'

'Money in advance.'

'Why?'

'In case we trash their caravans, I suppose. Where we're meant to sleep.'

'How much?

'Seventy pounds.' Then, when Rachel was about to yell at him, he said quickly, 'It's OK. I said we didn't have any money and they said it was OK and to come anyway.'

'But we've still got –' started Rachel.

'Shh. We'll hang on to that. We'll need to buy food.'

'So, what? I say we've got no money?'

Jack nodded. 'Yep.'

'OK,' she said uncertainly.

They stood around while people came and went, but no one took any notice of them. At last, when things had quietened down a bit, Jack approached one of the girls behind the tables.

'We've just arrived,' he said. 'Can you tell us what to do?'

She looked up at him with dead eyes. 'Name?'

'Jack Carter.'

'And your friend?'

Jack nudged Rachel. She jumped. 'Er. Rachel. Rachel Smith.'

The girl looked up. 'Sure it's Smith?'

Rachel blushed. 'Course I'm bloody sure!''

Jack shot her a warning look.

'Addresses,' said the bored girl.

For a moment, Jack hesitated, then he plucked an address out of his head.

'And her?' The girl nodded at Rachel.

Before Rachel could answer, Jack jumped in. 'She's my neighbour. Two doors down. Same street and everything, number sixty-four.'

Rachel opened her mouth to speak, then closed it again.

The girl looked up, the pen she'd been writing with twirling round slowly in her fingers. Jack held her grumpy stare and finally she dropped her gaze and started writing again.

At last she handed them a piece of paper. Jack stared at it. 'What do I do with this?'

The girl sighed and pointed to a group standing a little way off. There seemed to be some sort of dispute going on. Some young men were crowding round an older woman, gesticulating and gabbling in a foreign language.

'Show this to the woman over there.'

'What, the one taking all the abuse?' said Rachel.

'Yeah,' said the girl, 'and don't get lippy with her. She don't like it.'

Jack dragged Rachel away before she could answer back.

They hovered by the older woman but she ignored them, raising her voice to shout back at the young men.

'You know the deal. We keep the money till the season's finished. If you don't want the job, you can pack your bags. There're plenty more where you came from.'

She turned away from them, shrugging her shoulders.

Jack approached her. She frowned. 'Yes! What is it?' Her voice was sharp.

Silently, Jack showed her the piece of paper. She looked at it without interest. 'You the new ones?'

'Yes, we –' began Jack.

She cut him short, jerking her head at them to follow her.

'Bloody foreigners,' she muttered as they walked away. 'What do they expect?'

She took them across to another field where rows of caravans were parked.

'The others are full,' she said to Jack. 'But there's a space for you here.' She pointed at a mould-covered caravan with spongy tyres. 'Van twenty-three. Remember the number.'

'Can't we go in together?' asked Rachel.

'No. That's not how it works. Boys in together. Girls in together. Take it or leave it.'

'I don't want to share with some poxy girls,' whispered Rachel to Jack.

He shrugged. 'It's a roof, Rach,' he said.

'What did you call me?'

'Rach.'

She smiled suddenly. 'No one's called me that for ages.'

They peered into Jack's caravan. It had four berths and it smelled of unwashed bodies and fags. There were clothes on the floor and foil takeaway containers on the beds, half full of dried-up curry.

'Yuk!' said Rachel, but the woman didn't react. She turned, instead, to Jack.

'No smoking in the vans.'

Jack nodded.

As if anyone takes any notice.

Rachel's caravan was across the other side of the field. The inside wasn't much better. There was a girl lying on one of the beds, asleep, her arm flung back over her head. Rachel squinted round the door to get a look at her new roommate and took in the thick legs and short-cropped hair.

'God, I don't want to share with her.'

'Shh.'

'Washing and toilets over there,' said the woman, pointing to a breezeblock building in the far corner of the field. 'Dump your stuff and come to the barn when you're ready and someone will show you what to do.' Then she felt in the pocket of her jacket for a packet of fags and lit up before she started to walk away.

'What about food?' asked Jack.

She stopped and took a deep drag of her cigarette. 'You get your own,' she said. 'Walk into the village or get the bus. Goes in twice a day.'

'Right little ray of sunshine, isn't she?' said Rachel as she made faces at the woman's retreating back. 'What we doing here, Jack? It's horrible.'

Jack rounded on her, his temper suddenly flaring.

'Oh for God's sake, stop moaning at me! I'm doing my best.' He started to walk away, then shouted over his shoulder, 'I'll meet you back at the barn. I'm going to put my gear in the van, and go and have a wash.'

'I've got nothing to dump, only my handbag,' said Rachel.

'Well, don't leave money in it. Stuff the cash in your pocket.'

'I'm not daft,' she muttered. Then she added, 'There's hardly any left anyway.'

Later, they met up outside the barn. Rachel looked more cheerful.

'She's not bad, that big girl in my van,' she said. 'Called Yena, or something. Foreign. But she was friendly. Said she'd show me where to get the bus and stuff.'

Jack nodded. 'OK, we'll go and get food later.'

'And washing things. I haven't got nothing with me, remember.'

'Yes. OK. All that. Come on. There's still a bit of time before they knock off. We could make a start.'

Back at the barn they were given trays and punnets and told what to do.

It was hard work, bending down between the rows of strawberries, picking the ripe fruit, filling the punnets, filling the trays, then going back to the barn for weighing and collecting their slip for payment.

Jack picked the fruit steadily but Rachel soon got bored. She kept stopping, standing up, jiggling from one foot to the other. Jack noticed that she often scratched her arms and that there was a fine sheen of sweat on her face.

'My back aches. I hate doing this.'

Jack bit back a sarcastic comment. 'It's money, Rach,' he said.

'Huh, not much, is it?'

Jack was tired and sweating and his back ached too.

'For Chrissake, Rachel. Man up, will you?'

'Huh, that's rich, coming from you!'

Jack straightened up and looked at her. 'What do you mean?'

'Nothing,' muttered Rachel.

Jack didn't reply but bent down again and continued picking.

Rachel stood still for a minute, then she bent down beside him.

'Sorry.'

He didn't answer.

Rachel started picking again.

At knocking off time, they went to the barn and stood in a queue with their slips. When they handed them over, one of the dead-eyed girls looked at it and noted something down.

'Next,' she said.

'Where's our money?' said Rachel.

The bored girl hardly glanced at her. 'You gotta work off the rent for the van and the deposit first,' she said.

'What? I've gotta pay for sleeping in that poxy van?'

The girl shrugged and turned away.

Rachel opened her mouth to yell something at the girl but Jack pulled her away.

'It won't take long,' he said quietly. He pointed to a notice stuck on the side of the barn. 'It says what the rent is here – and the deposit. Should only take us a couple of days to earn that if we work fast, then, after a few weeks you'll have enough money to get to London and find somewhere to live.'

Rachel rolled her eyes at him. 'That long? Jeez, Jack, I'm knackered already.'

A boy in the crowd heard her. 'It gets easier,' he said, smiling. 'The first week, that is bad. Then it is better.'

Jack recognised him as one of the foreign pickers who had been arguing with the woman earlier. He turned to him. 'How long you been here?' he asked.

'Two weeks,' said the boy, his English stilted and formal. He stuck out his hand. 'My name's Raffi.'

'I'm Jack – and this is Rachel.'

Rachel looked Raffi up and down. 'He's well fit,' she whispered to Jack.

'We go into the village now,' said Raffi, indicating some of the other pickers standing nearby. 'For food. You want to come with us? The bus goes in twenty minutes.'

'Sure,' said Rachel, suddenly brightening. Jack looked at her but said nothing.

A group of them set off for the village. Raffi and his friends seemed friendly enough. They told Jack and Rachel that they'd come from Romania on a scheme organised by some of the guys who ran the farm. They'd arranged it all for them.

'How does that work, then? asked Jack. 'Did you have to pay them?'

'Yes,' said Raffi, looking away.

Something in his expression made Jack stop asking any more questions. The group fell silent, then, until the bus reached the village.

There was a mini supermarket in the village. Jack automatically looked round to see if there was any out of date food in bins round the back but he couldn't spot anything. He and Rachel bought enough food to last a couple of days and some toiletries for Rachel.

'They charge a bloody fortune,' whispered Rachel.

'Yeah, I know. But there's nowhere else.'

'Did you nick anything?'

'I *told* you, I only do that when I have to.'

On the way back to the farm they talked some

more to Raffi and his friends. Raffi asked which vans they were sleeping in.

'Mine's twenty-three,' said Jack.

Raffi looked up sharply. He turned to his friends. They shook their heads and started talking in their own language.

'What are they saying?' asked Jack.

Raffi looked uncomfortable. 'Nothing. It is nothing.'

Rachel stared at him. 'Yes it is. What is it? Who's in number twenty-three?'

Raffi shrugged. 'The guys in there . . .'

'What?' said Rachel. 'What's wrong with them?'

But Raffi wouldn't be drawn. He turned to Jack. 'Be careful,' he said.

Jack felt a twist of fear in his gut, the same feeling he'd had when he'd been trapped in his bedroom at home and heard the footsteps on the stairs, willing them not to stop at his door, knowing he had nowhere to go, that there was no escape.

Rachel and Jack ate with the others when they returned to the farm. Jack got up afterwards and walked over to his van. He was dreading what he would find and he wanted to face up to the men in there before his imagination got out of hand, but when he pushed open the door, there was no one else there. The tinfoil containers of half-eaten Indian meals were still lying on the beds, so he went back and found Rachel.

She was sitting a little apart from Raffi and his friends, and he saw the change in her at once. Her whole body language was different, her limbs relaxed and still. She looked up when he approached and gave him a lazy smile, her pupils small pinpoints in her eyes.

Oh God, someone's given her drugs. Stupid, stupid girl.

He sat down heavily beside her. She was the first to break the silence and her voice was slurred.

'Jack, you know when you said about those allot-thingies?'

It took him a moment to understand what she was talking about.

'You mean the allotments? The place where we spent the night?'

She nodded and then drew up her knees, hugging them to her chest.

'How did you know they were there? Had you been there before or something?'

'I told you,' he said, his voice tight with the anger in him. Who had supplied her? What had she taken?

'Oh yeah. Some story about your mum's friend.'

He didn't bother to answer. Had she picked up on the uncertainty? He had sort of remembered it, and he may have gone there before but that didn't explain the clarity with which he'd seen the allotments in his mind's eye, been drawn to them.

Rachel leaned into him. 'Do you see things, Jack?'

What's this? Can she read my mind now?

'What do you mean?' he said carefully.

She giggled. 'I see things.'

His patience snapped. 'Yeah, sure you see things, Rachel. Especially when you're stoned out of your skull.'

'Why are you so horrible? I thought you were my friend.'

Jack moved away from her.

'What, so you're going to give up on me too?' Her voice was getting louder.

'Who supplied you Rachel? Where did you get the stuff from?'

She started sniffing. 'I'm not telling. Anyway, it's only weed. It makes me feel better. It helps send the voices away.'

He frowned. 'The voices?'

She seemed to sober up in an instant, stiffening beside him.

'Do you hear voices, Rachel? Like voices in your head?'

She didn't answer but started to pick at her T-shirt.

'Do you?' he persisted.

'Forget it.'

'Tell me.'

She shook her head. 'It's private.'

'You can tell me.'

'You'll laugh at me.'

'Try me.'

She turned away from him so she couldn't see his face, couldn't judge his expression.

'I hear things . . .' she began.

He didn't say anything and she continued, hesitating, not knowing how to tell him, not having the words.

'People talk to me.'

'In your head?'

She nodded. 'Yeah.' Then it came out all in a rush. 'And a tune, there's always a tune.'

Jack turned towards her.

'See, I knew you'd rubbish me,' she said, when he still didn't speak.

'I'm not rubbishing you.' He paused. 'These voices. Have you always heard them?'

'I've heard the voices since I was little.' Her voice was very quiet.

'And are they always there?'

She nodded. 'They get louder sometimes.'

'When you're in trouble?'

'Yeah, when I'm in deep shit.'

She got up and started to stamp her feet. 'It's getting cold. Think I'll go back to me van.'

'Rach.'

'Yeah?'

'Do you think it's . . .'

'What? Think it's what?'

'No. Forget it. Nothing.'

She turned back to him then. 'If you're thinking it's the drugs, you're wrong. I heard the voices long before I ever . . . Oh forget it. I shouldn't've said anything. You just think I'm daft.' And, when he didn't reply, she added, 'I'm off now. I'm bloody knackered.'

Jack sat where he was. He watched until she was swallowed up in the gloom.

Weird. He'd heard of people hearing voices in their head but he'd never really believed it.

He started walking slowly across the field towards van twenty-three, Raffi's words sounding in his head. *Be careful.*

His stomach clenched. The other occupants were sure to be back by now but he couldn't put it off for ever.

All three were there in the van. As he opened the door, the smell of fags, beer and curry came at him in a great wave, making his eyes smart.

'Hi,' Jack murmured.

One of the men looked up. 'Close the door,' he said gruffly.

Jack closed the door. He saw that his backpack had been moved from one of the beds and had been tossed on the floor of the van. One of the straps was broken.

They've been through my stuff.

He said nothing but picked it up and looked inside it. There was nothing there worth stealing – he had no money after all – but everything had been messed up.

The men watched him silently, then one of them slid off a top bunk and dropped close to Jack. 'Wassyer name?' he asked.

Not Eastern Europeans, then. This guy was English, though Jack couldn't immediately place the accent.

'Jack.'

'OK, Jack. You get that one.' He pointed up to the other top bunk.

Jack nodded silently.

One of the other men, a short guy with several days' stubble on his chin and greasy black hair, sat up in one of the lower bunks.

'Want a game of cards, Jack?'

He knew what that meant.

'No, I've not got any cash.'

'Who said anything about cash?' said greasy hair. 'Put it on the slate.'

Jack shook his head. 'I'm bushed,' he said. 'I'm going to bed.'

'I'm bushed. I'm going to bed,' mimicked the first man.

Damn my accent.

Jack said nothing and started to climb up to his bunk, dragging his backpack with him. The other man in the van had so far said nothing, just looked Jack up and down, grunted and then lain back, taking another drag on his cigarette.

There was very little headspace between the bunk and the ceiling of the van, and only a couple of old blankets. Jack noticed that the others had pillows but he wasn't about to argue. He took off his jacket, crawled under the blankets and used his backpack as a pillow. He was so shattered that despite the mutterings, laughing of the men and the smoke that drifted up and constricted his chest, he slept almost immediately.

He woke once during the night, desperate for a pee and his chest tight, so he lowered himself, as quietly as he could, down to the floor and crept out of the door. It was still dark but it was a summer dark, never impenetrable like the night skies in the depth of winter. He peed on the grass then stood outside for a while listening, thinking of Rachel, a girl with so many issues. Scared of the countryside, frightened of animal noises and rustlings and the silence. Scared of everything and masking it with rudeness and drugs. But maybe, beneath it all, there was some shred of what might have been if she'd been dealt a better hand.

But what was it?

He took some deep breaths before going into the

van again to face the fetid, stale smells and the snores of the men, then he opened the door quietly, crept inside and hauled himself up to his bunk. The man below him grunted and turned over but didn't wake.

Rachel

before

It didn't matter to begin with. I was too little to know. Thought everyone lived in care. Thought it was normal. And I soon learned to fight my own corner. All the kids there had issues – well, of course they did. I only ever made one friend. Tracey. She was a right laugh and we hung out from when we were little. It was Rach and Trace against the world. Right cheeky little sods, we were. But I was sort of happy then. Trace always understood, even when things were really bad, and she was always there for me. We'd giggle about all the ologists they sent to talk to us. They had to do it, had to fill in all the forms, tick all the boxes. It was all rubbish. Me and Trace'd either tell them a pack of lies or try to second guess them; we always knew what they wanted to hear.

Then Trace got moved on. Got fostered. She was shit scared when she left the home. I sat up all night talking to her about the new family. She said they seemed OK, but how could she tell? And it was bloody miles away from the home. We swore to keep in touch, we even cut ourselves and mixed our blood. 'Now we're blood sisters,' she'd said. She sent me a letter once. She was better at me than writing and that but I couldn't make it out. I hid that I couldn't read and I didn't want the others to know, so I never knew what she said in her letter. I've kept it, though. I've still got it.

It was a nightmare going to school. Even in primary they were cruel; they soon sussed out you were in care. They gave me some special teacher to help me but I couldn't learn. The letters were just a jumble. That's when I started kicking off. Shouting and screaming so they'd leave me in peace.

Chapter 5

In the morning, the others were awake before him. Greasy-hair shook him.

'Get up, lad. Time for breakfast.'

In the daylight, the men looked less threatening and Jack learned their names.

Greasy-hair was called Mike and the other two were Cam and Tyler. Mike and Cam weren't friendly exactly, more indifferent, but Tyler ignored him completely and only spoke once – when Jack bumped into him in the close confines of the van.

'Watch it,' he said, and shoved Jack so violently that he fell back and bruised his shoulder on the woodwork.

The dew was still on the grass as Jack walked over the field to the van where Rachel was sleeping. He could hear movement inside and he banged on the door. One of the other girls poked her head out.

'You Rachel's friend?'

Jack nodded, though he wasn't sure if friend was the right word.

There was some swearing from inside.

'Bloody hell it's too crowded in 'ere. I can't find me knickers.'

Eventually, Rachel emerged, laughing, followed by the other girls.

There was a building with some basic cooking facilities and they all made their way over there. Rachel had hung on to the food they'd bought – *Just as well,* thought Jack, *that lot in my van would've had it off me* – and they stood in line to fry up their eggs and bread and brew some tea.

'What are the blokes like in your van?' asked Rachel.

Jack made a face. 'Bit rough.'

'Girls in mine are a right laugh,' said Rachel. 'They're OK.'

As they were eating their food, Mike came over to them. He bent down and whispered something in Jack's ear and Jack nodded.

'What did he say?' asked Rachel.

Jack waited until he was out of earshot.

'Just warning me.'

'What about?'

'Told me not to make Tyler angry.'

'Who's Tyler?'

'One of the guys in the van. He's a moody sod. I wouldn't like to get on the wrong side of him.'

'Better keep your head down, then.'

'Yep.'

By the time they broke for lunch, Rachel had had enough.

'I can't stand no more of this,' she moaned. 'My back's killing me and my feet hurt and I need a fix. I've had it with this place.'

It was a warm summer's day and they were sitting together, sharing their food, propped up against the wheels of the tractor that ferried the pallets of strawberries away from the farm.

Jack was tired too. 'Stop moaning, Rachel. Everyone's tired. And we've got to pay off the deposit and the van rent, remember? And,' he added, 'we're not going to save any money if you spend it on –'

'All right! Stop going on at me.' She paused and looked round. 'I hate it here.'

'Oh shut it. Go back to Adam, then.'

Jack got up and moved away. He sat down by a tree that had a good view of the fields, which sloped down gently towards the river at the bottom. He took out his sketchpad and a pencil from his jacket pocket and started to draw. He focused on his drawing, forgetting his aching back, forgetting the men in van twenty-three, forgetting Rachel, absorbed in what he was doing. For a while, he was able to forget everything except what he saw – the heat haze, the figures moving slowly down the rows of strawberries, the line of trees in the distance along the river's edge.

He was so caught up in his work that he didn't hear her creep up behind him. She sniffed as she peered over his shoulder.

'Hey, that's effing brilliant, Jack.'

Slowly, he came out of his trance, turned and looked at her. Was this her way of saying sorry? He smiled, carefully closing the sketchpad and putting it back in his jacket pocket.

'Better get picking,' he said.

'No, I'm going back to the van for a rest,' said Rachel.

Jack caught her arm. 'No you're bloody not,' he said. 'We've got to keep going, earn some money. We agreed.'

'But I'm tired.'

'So am I.'

They glared at each other, then Rachel dropped her eyes. 'Why does everyone always shout at me?'

Because you irritate the hell out of them.

Jack sighed. 'Come on, Rach,' he said. 'Everyone says the first few days are the worst. After that you get used to it.'

They trailed back to the fields, Rachel sniffing and complaining at every step. Then suddenly she stopped.

'That drawing,' she said.

'What about it?'

'That's, like, proper drawing. You could sell it.'

Jack smiled. 'I thought that once . . .'

Back in the day it might have been possible, when the art teacher, the one person who had encouraged him at that dreadful school, had said he had talent, could go far, must go to art school and get proper training. Back then he'd thought maybe . . .

'I can't do nothing like that,' said Rachel.

Was it his job to encourage her?

'Bet you can do *something*.'

Rachel shrugged. 'I used to like singing, but then . . .'

'What sort of singing?'

'Pop songs and stuff. Once someone showed me a few chords on a guitar, but I was crap at it. I'm crap at everything.'

They had reached their strawberry row and Jack stopped, shrugged off his backpack and crouched down. 'Raffi and his mates have got a guitar,' he said, over his shoulder.

Rachel slithered to a stop behind him. 'Hey, d'you think . . . ? Nah, I'd be no good, anyway.'

Jack didn't answer. He was already busy picking.

Rachel watched him for a few moments. 'Why don't you leave your backpack in the van?' she said.

'Why do you think?'

'You scared those blokes'll nick it?'

Jack nodded. 'They'd nick anything.'

Rachel squatted down in the row beside him and started picking. After a while, she began humming, quietly at first and then more loudly.

'What's that tune, Rach? It's nice.'

She didn't answer and when he looked over at her she was staring straight ahead, her hands idle and her eyes focused on something he couldn't see. He stopped picking for a moment and watched and listened. She didn't notice him, seemed unaware of his presence. The sound of her voice, as the hum transformed itself into words, was pure and beautiful, an effortless sound.

Pure and beautiful, he thought and grinned. Not words he'd associate with Rachel.

Still smiling, he went back to work. After a while, Rachel stopped singing, looked around her in confusion, then down at the strawberry plants.

'Have one of your turns, did you?' asked Jack.

'What?'

He didn't meet her eyes. 'Hearing your voices?'

'Yeah,' she said shortly.

'Want to tell me about it?'

She shook her head and bent down again, her long

bleached hair flopping over her face. Jack could see an inch of dark hair growing through.

The days went by and they got into a sort of routine. By the end of the second week they'd paid off their deposit and started earning a bit of money. Jack never went anywhere without his cash; he didn't dare leave it in the van. The men tolerated him, but only just, and if they'd been drinking he lay awake in his bunk bed, scared of what might happen.

After the first few days when Rachel was constantly moaning and talking about leaving, she began to settle down and as soon as they were earning, she gave her money to Jack for safekeeping.

'Why?' he asked.

'Why d'you think?'

'Does this mean . . . ?'

'Yeah, it does. I'm trying, OK?'

If she didn't have money, she couldn't buy weed. She never said it out loud, but he understood.

It was a breakthrough of sorts.

A few days later she said, out of nowhere, 'You're a funny sod, Jack, but I trust you.'

He stopped what he was doing and smiled at her. She frowned. 'So don't bloody let me down.'

Jack turned away from her so she couldn't see his expression.

Sometimes she picked beside him and sometimes with the girls in her van. She was a rotten picker, often getting bored and sloping off somewhere, but even she could see that the more she picked, the more money she earned.

Jack, meanwhile, picked steadily, sometimes teaming up with Raffi and his mates. He liked Raffi and they would often take their lunch break together. Raffi told Jack about his life in Romania, about how he was trying to earn money for his family back there and about his hopes for the future.

'But it is hard,' said Raffi, looking up into the distance. 'This work is not . . .'

'It's a lot of work for not much money,' agreed Jack.

But Raffi shook his head. 'No,' he said slowly. 'No, you don't understand.'

Jack twisted round to look at him. 'What is it?'

'It is not your problem.' Raffi shrugged.

Jack frowned. He had noticed that Raffi and his friends never received any money at the end of the week.

'Are you not being paid?'

'We are being paid,' said Raffi slowly. 'But only very little.'

'So, the guy who set this up for you gets most of it? Is that what you're saying?'

Raffi nodded. 'He says we will get our money at the finish of the season, but I don't believe him.'

'Doesn't he give you any money?'

'Just enough for food. No more.'

'But that's really bad, Raffi. Can't you complain?'

Raffi shrugged again. 'We have tried, my friend. But they are all in it together. It is, what you call it? A scam.'

'Who are these guys?'

'The people who run this place.' He hesitated, and suddenly Jack knew what he was leaving unsaid.

'It's those guys in my van, isn't it? They're part of it.'

Raffi nodded. 'Yes,' he said quietly. 'They are part of it. That's why I told you to be careful.'

'I wondered why I'd never seen them picking,' said Jack.

Raffi shook his head. 'No,' he said quietly. 'I guess they make enough money from us poor foreigners. I know they won't give us all the money we are due at the end of the season.'

'I'm really sorry, Raffi. You've been a good friend. I wish I could help.'

For the rest of the day, Jack kept thinking about how Cam and the others were stealing most of Raffi's earnings and it made him so furious that he was slow and clumsy at his picking. That evening he told Rachel what was happening.

'Those effing thugs!' she said. 'They're just a bunch of crims!'

It was not long after this that the dog appeared. It was a strange-looking creature, stick thin, its ribs showing through its rough, cream-coloured coat. It had a long nose, a wonky ear and great long skinny legs. It squeezed through the fence and made straight for Jack.

He stopped picking and sat back on his haunches, putting out his hand to stroke it. 'Hey, here boy.'

The dog licked his hand, sat down beside him and scratched.

All morning it stayed by his side and when they broke for lunch, Jack gave it a bit of bread and then led it over to the water trough to have a drink.

Rachel was nearby. 'Watch it,' she said. 'You'll never get rid of the thing if you feed it. It's just a rotten flea-bitten stray.'

Jack smiled. 'Bit like us, then, isn't it?'

'Look, we got enough trouble looking after ourselves; we don't want no bleeding dog tagging along.'

But Jack bought tins of dog food from the village and, over the next few days, the dog began to look less scrawny. Everywhere Jack went, it followed him and after a while, even Rachel accepted its presence.

'What sort of dog is it, then?'

Jack frowned, looking at its long nose and fragile legs. 'I dunno. Some sort of greyhound cross, I guess.'

He often drew it in his sketchbook. Lively, funny

drawings of the dog scratching or stretched out, its head on its forepaws, or bounding after a butterfly, its ears flapping.

One day after work, Jack and Rachel went into the village with Raffi and his friends. This time they walked there and back, the dog at their heels. In the supermarket, Rachel kept picking up stuff they couldn't afford.

'Put that back, Rach. We've got to try to save some money.'

'You're buying all that dog food – why can't I have this?' she said, waving a bottle of cheap perfume at him, but she soon replaced it on the shelves.

Later they ate together with Raffi and the others, and some of the girls in Rachel's van came and joined them. One of Raffi's friends brought a guitar along and they sang some songs. At first, Rachel sat silently, staring at the guitar and just mouthing some of the words, absently reaching down to stroke the rough coat of the dog which was curled up beside Jack.

Jack nudged her. 'Go on, Rach, join in.'

She shook her head, so Jack started singing instead.

'You're a crap singer,' she said, putting her hands over her ears and laughing.

'OK. Want to show me how it's done, then?'

She started humming, then, when she could remember the words, joining in with some of the lyrics.

Raffi's mate started another song.

Rachel, who had been slumped against Jack's back, sat up straight.

'Hey, I know this one,' she said. 'I used to sing it back when . . .'

'Go on, then,' whispered Jack.

Rachel closed her eyes and began singing. Quietly at first and then with more confidence.

As her voice rose above the others, there was a gradual change of mood in the group. Before, not everyone had been listening to the singing – there had been chatter and background noise going on – but as Rachel continued, the other noises fell away and, one by one, the others stopped singing or talking and listened. Raffi's friend changed his playing too. He was following her voice now, no longer belting out the chords but playing softly, accompanying her.

As she sang, Rachel seemed unaware of the people around her. She was completely taken over by the music. Her eyes were closed, her voice rising and falling, instinctively putting expression into the lyrics. When the song ended and the last chord faded away, she slowly opened her eyes.

There was a moment's silence – and then everyone clapped.

Raffi's friend with the guitar was staring at her. 'How did you learn to sing like that?' he asked.

Rachel looked down at the ground. 'I never learned,' she said.

Everyone was crowding round her now, congratulating her. Embarrassed, she turned to Jack. He was staring at her.

'That was awesome, Rach.'

That's why. Now I understand. That's why she's my mark!

She smiled at him then; a genuine smile that lit up her face.

Raffi's friend came over. 'Hey, you should learn to play the guitar,' he said.

He sat down beside her and placed the fingers of her left hand on the fret.

'See, if you place this finger here, and this one here – and here. Press down firmly, then draw your thumb across the strings.'

Jack watched her face. She was concentrating in a way he'd never seen her concentrate before.

This is what lights her up.

She was frowning, pressing her fingers down on the strings and then drawing her thumb down.

'Yes, yes, that's right.'

'That's C, isn't it?'

He nodded. 'Yes, that's the chord of C.'

'I remember that one.'

Jack went on watching her. When had that happened?

And who had taught her? Had there once been a time in her life when someone cared enough to bother? He'd never seen her concentrate on anything for so long. Usually she was bored in seconds, but he could see she was really engaged. It was a Rachel he didn't recognise.

She has a talent. Who would have thought it?

Why? Why shouldn't she be talented? some other part of him argued. *Just because you've put her in some stupid box labelled* dumb blonde.

It was getting late. The others in the group began to drift away but Rachel and the guitarist remained sitting, heads bent, going over and over the chords, and he was humming some simple tunes to go with them. They were still totally absorbed.

It suddenly hit him. He could leave now. She'd be OK. She could hang out with Raffi and Yelena and he could slip away. The time felt right. He mustn't get any deeper in.

But still something was holding him there.

Rachel's bag was lying on the grass and he took out the phone. God, it was on! How had that happened? They'd been so careful since they'd been here, not used it in case Adam had some GPS app and was tracking them. Had Rachel shown it to someone, let them use it? How could she have been so stupid? Jack pressed *messages* and saw that there was a recent text. Very recent.

How's life at the fruit farm, you bitch?

Instantly, he turned it off. His stomach spasmed and he suddenly felt cold. He held the phone in his hand for a moment. Hell! They'd been right; all this time Adam had been trying to track them through the phone. And he'd just found out where they were; typically stupid of him, though, to boast about it, give them warning.

Not for the first time, Jack wondered why Adam was so desperate to find Rachel. After all, there were other girls.

Jack shivered and put the phone in his pocket. His mouth was dry. He swallowed, then he touched Rachel's arm. She didn't notice so he did it again, pulling it away from the guitar.

'Rach!' he said urgently.

'Leave me alone, will you!'

'Rach, I've got to talk to you.' He waved the phone in front of her face. She frowned and focused on him. As soon as he had her attention, he whispered into her ear. 'It's Adam. You left the phone on; he knows where we are. He must've got some fancy tracking app.'

She dropped the guitar. Raffi's friend picked it up. 'Careful,' he said.

'Sorry. I'm sorry. I've gotta go.' She scrambled to her feet, looking around her into the evening twilight.

'What's the hurry? You were doing really well,' said the boy.

Rachel turned to him. 'Thanks,' she said. 'Thanks for that. It was . . . it was great.'

Then, without a backward glance, she followed Jack and the dog away, across the field, until they were sure no one could hear them.

'When did he send the message?' she asked.

'About half an hour ago.'

'Oh God, I'm sorry. I forgot. I let Raffi make a call on it. His phone needed charging. Does that mean . . .?'

Jack nodded. 'Yeah. If he's coming in his car, I guess he could be here any time.'

'Shit!' Rachel was shaking and trying not to cry. 'I like it here,' she whispered. 'It's hard work but the girls are a laugh – and that guy with the guitar . . .' She trailed off.

'I know. You were great, Rach.'

She took a deep, shuddering breath. 'The voices – they went away when I was singing. Really went away.'

'Oh, Rach.'

She sniffed.

Jack bit his lip. 'Maybe Adam's only bluffing,' he said. 'Maybe he's just trying to scare you.'

'Adam doesn't do bluffing,' she said bitterly.

Jack frowned. 'He's gone to a lot of trouble to track you down. Have you got something on him? Is that why he's so keen to find you?'

'I dunno. At first I thought he just wanted me back

for his . . . you know, the men . . . but maybe it's not just that.'

'What else?'

Rachel started chewing her nails. 'There could be something else.'

'Something you know about him?'

She nodded into the darkness. 'I overheard him talking to this guy once. I was so into Adam I didn't think much about it then – and I guess I was too stoned to really take it in, but . . .'

'What?'

'I'm thinking clearer now and I keep playing it over in my head.' There was a pause, then she said, 'Jack, I think I know something really bad about him.'

'What could be worse than what he's doing already? That's bad enough.'

'This is worse. I think that's why he's trying to find me. He wants to have me under his control, or . . .'

'Or?'

'Or get rid of me,' she said. But she spoke so quietly that Jack didn't hear. She cleared her throat. 'What are we going to do?'

Jack no longer questioned the *we*.

How had it happened? Gradually he'd got used to her, been surprised by her. At first he'd resented her, resented feeling he had to look out for someone so dumb and needy, yet bit by bit she had insinuated herself into his life; she was growing on him and he'd begun to think of them as a couple. He smiled to himself. Well, not *that* sort of couple, but two rudderless souls up against the world.

He took a deep breath. 'Either we run away again or we stay and face him.'

'We?' She gave him a weak smile. 'You're not gonna leave me, then?'

'I'll stay as long as I can.'

What else could he say?

'We could go to London now,' she said. 'We've got a bit of money.'

Not enough.

Jack swallowed. 'Or you could report Adam to the police,' he said slowly.

As long as I'm not mentioned.

Rachel's head shot up. 'Not that again. I told you, no police.'

Jack pulled at his ear. 'Rach, did you have sex with him?'

'None of your business. Why you asking?'

'It's just . . . well, it's not legal. You know, underage sex. You could report him for that.'

She rounded on him then, her eyes hard. 'When have the police ever listened to me? When all that other stuff happened, they never believed me then, did they? Look, I don't trust them.'

'What other stuff?'

She started to chew at her thumbnail. 'I don't want to talk about it, OK? I want to forget all that.'

'OK.' He went on, thinking aloud, 'Anyway, if you did that, you'd have to make statements and stuff.'

'And go to court,' said Rachel.

Jack looked at her. 'You've been there before, haven't you?'

'Yeah. I've been there before. And I'd be back in the system – social workers, care, same old, same old.'

They were silent for a bit. It was a lot cooler now. Jack pulled his jacket round him and shivered.

'What would Adam do, if he came here?'

Rachel shook her head. 'He'd get his guys to force me into his car.'

'But someone would stop him. I'd stop him.'

She laughed. 'My hero, eh? You wouldn't stand a chance.'

'Everyone else too,' he said weakly.

She shrugged. 'He'd tell lies about me. Say I'm his kid sister or something. Look, this lot here, they don't want no trouble, do they? They don't want no runaway girl. They'd be glad to see the back of me.'

Runaway girl. Were people out looking for her, then? Not just Adam, but the social services guys? Did they really care that much?

Jack thrust his hands deep into the pockets of his

jacket. 'We haven't got much money, Rach. Not enough to survive in London for long.'

'You could steal some more,' she said.

Jack thought of the men in his van. He knew where they put the money. One night, when he was pretending to be asleep, he'd seen them thumbing through the notes and then stuffing them back deep down into a pillowcase. By rights, most of that money belonged to Raffi and his mates. But if Tyler caught him . . . He closed his eyes, hearing the sound of the footsteps on the stairs again. Still a part of his nightmares, and of his guilt.

Stop it. Don' t go there.

'That's a crap idea,' he said.

Rachel started to cry. 'Things were getting better . . .'

'I know.'

Rachel sniffed and wiped her nose on her sleeve. 'What are we going to do?'

'We can't do anything tonight. We'll leave as soon as it gets light.'

'But if Adam comes . . .'

Jack hesitated. 'I think we'll have to risk it. I don't think he'll come now. It's dark. He wouldn't know where to look, would he? He wouldn't know which van you're in and there'd be no one around to ask.'

'I want to go now,' said Rachel. 'I'm scared.'

'Rach, it's too late. We'll get up really early.'

They walked back to Rachel's van. 'I won't sleep,' she said.

Jack turned and went back to van twenty-three. He wouldn't sleep either. When he reached the van, he hesitated before opening the door. He had to psyche himself up to go in.

He stooped down to pat the dog, which was padding silently beside him. The dog licked his hand and then wriggled underneath the van.

They'd been drinking. He could smell the booze. The three of them were slouched over the little table, smoking and playing cards.

Tyler looked up, his eyes bleary and his big forehead beaded with sweat. 'Look who's here. Our pretty boy, Jack. Gonna come and join us, then?'

It was a threat.

Jack swallowed. 'I told you, I haven't got any money.'

Mike leaned back. 'Don't you lie to us, Jack. You're earning now.'

Jack had thought that Mike was the friendliest of the three of them but full of booze and with the others for support, he was just as threatening.

They all turned to look at Jack then. His mouth was dry and his heart was hammering in his chest but he said evenly, 'No thanks,' and started to climb up to his bunk. Just as he was swinging his leg over to get on top of it, Tyler rose to his feet, lurched over and pulled

Jack's leg so that he had to grab onto the wooden rails to stop himself from crashing down to the floor. He gasped with the shock of it, then felt Tyler's arms round him, lifting him down and dumping him on the floor.

Tyler wrenched the pack off his back and dumped it by the door.

'Coming to play now?' he asked.

They all looked at him then, smirking. Jack made a grab for the door handle but Tyler shoved him out of the way.

'Sneaky little poof,' he said, holding him fast.

Jack let himself go limp. He knew he couldn't fight back. His only chance was to pretend to agree, to go along with them.

Tyler pushed him towards the table, laughing. 'Come on, pretty boy. Cam, deal him out the cards.'

As they made room for him, Tyler released him. Jack began to sit down, then he suddenly twisted away, grabbed his backpack from beside the door and made another grab for the door handle. This time he was there before they moved, all clumsy with drink, and flung himself out into the night.

He heard their shouts follow him. 'Hey, Jack. Come on. We'll have some fun here.' Then laughter and a shout from Tyler. 'Nowhere to sleep out there, pretty boy. You go and find that slag girlfriend of yours. No use to her, are you?'

Jack ran as fast as he could, just to get away from them. He couldn't spend another night there. He stopped when his chest hurt too much for him to continue and he stood, close to the toilet block, doubled over, gasping for breath.

Thank God he still had his backpack with him. He felt in his pocket for Rachel's phone. He took it out and then, without looking at it, chucked it into the bushes.

He breathed in the country air. He felt like crying and the tears began to well up.

Stop it! Think.

He sat back on his haunches and swore. Running. Always running. Away from trouble, away from his demons. That's what it had been like before. Before it had happened. He didn't want to go back there.

There was someone coming towards the toilet block. Jack froze, then relaxed when he saw who it was.

'Raffi!'

Raffi whipped round and peered into the shadows, then when his eyes adjusted to the dark, he let out his breath.

'Jack, what are you doing? You scared me.'

'Sorry, mate.' Jack stood up.

Raffi came closer. 'What is it, Jack? Is it those men?'

Jack nodded into the darkness. 'I can't stay in that van,' he said. 'You've no idea.'

Raffi gave a humourless laugh. 'Oh, yes, I do.'

'Can I stay in your van?'

'Sure.'

Jack waited for Raffi to use the toilet and then they went back to his van together. Jack lay down on the floor between the bunks, using his backpack as a pillow. Raffi found him a blanket.

He listened to the sounds of the others in the van, the light snores, the mumblings, the tossing and turning. He knew he wouldn't be able to sleep but at least he was under shelter. And with friends.

By the time dawn came, he'd made up his mind.

Jack

before

It was just the four of us then, Mum and me and the twins, and the elephant in the room: Dad's presence. The twins had each other and they were little; they seemed to miss him less. But for me, his presence was sometimes so strong I could feel it, specially when I was doing something like playing sport. I wasn't very good at sport, not like him, but I quite enjoyed it. I knew he'd been disappointed when I didn't make the school teams but he'd never said anything, just kept encouraging me. With him gone I played less and less sport; I'd only done it because he was so keen. I was more like Mum and she encouraged me with my drawing, even said she could see I had talent. But then, she was my mum, wasn't she? Of course she'd say that.

I went through the motions, passed exams, spoke when I was spoken to, had some friends. Not close friends really because they did different things, but it was OK – sort of.

We functioned, the four of us, and got back into some sort of normal routine. We never ever forgot Dad but the hole he left began, slowly, to get smaller. Sometimes I'd see something – a photo, a backpack, the big gnarled old stick he'd used for hill walking – just little things, and it would hit me again, knocking the breath out of me.

And then Mum met Kevin.

Chapter 6

He left the dog sleeping under Raffi's van.

He'd been planning to head straight over to Rachel's van but something made him hesitate and he found himself going towards van twenty-three. He tried to turn back but whatever it was that was propelling him was too strong to resist and he was at the familiar door, reaching for the handle.

What am I doing here?

But he knew what he was doing, why he was there, and he was scared shitless.

Very softly he turned the handle and opened the door.

It's no good, he thought. *It won't be there. I won't be able to get it.*

Still, his body moved forward. The door was wide enough open, now, for him to mount the steps and creep inside. He hesitated, his heart racing. He felt so sick that it took him a moment to focus.

They were all still asleep. Tyler, in his bottom bunk, was lying on his back with his arms dangling over the edge, snoring steadily.

It will be behind his head, thought Jack. *I'll never be able to get at it without disturbing him.*

He looked around, conscious that, at any moment, one of them might wake up and see him, conscious of his heart beating wildly against his ribcage, terrified that his chest would spasm and he'd have to cough.

And then he saw it. Tyler's pillow.

It must have slipped off during the night. It was lying on the floor between the bunks.

Jack crept forward, pausing when the unstable van swayed under his weight. Then he went down on all fours and crawled towards the pillow. He didn't dare look up, hardly dared to breathe.

He'd reached it now. Very slowly, he pushed his hand down between the pillow and the pillowcase, right to the bottom.

At first he thought he'd been mistaken. That this wasn't the hiding place, but then his hand felt something solid at the bottom. Wads of notes, several of them, kept together by elastic bands.

Just take one, he told himself. His fingers closed round one of the bulky wads and he started, very carefully, to withdraw it. Bit by bit, watching Tyler's sleeping form all the time, he took it out and started crawling back towards the door.

There was a sudden groan from one of the bunks and Jack froze. The noise had come from one of the other men, in a top bunk. Jack stared up and saw the mattress move as he turned over and groaned again. Tyler stopped snoring for a moment. Still Jack dared not move. He waited. Then, at last, Tyler started snoring once more, and very, very slowly, Jack shuffled back, a few centimetres at a time, until he reached the open door. He slid his body down the steps and, pausing only to close the van door as quietly as he could, he ran for Raffi's van.

He crept inside and shook Raffi's sleeping form. He took an age to wake up.

'Jack?'

'Raffi, I've got something for you.'

Raffi sat up and stared at Jack as he thrust the wad of notes at him.

'It's yours, mate. It's what Tyler stole from you. I'm going now and he'll know I've taken it. He won't suspect you.'

'Jack, I –'

'Don't say anything, mate. It's yours. It belongs to you and the others. You've earned it.'

As he left, Jack wondered, briefly, why he'd not taken some for himself. But he knew why: that money was Raffi's. Not his. He and Rachel would have to get by on what they had.

He was soon at Rachel's van, banging on it, chilled with fear and lack of sleep. He saw her peer out of the window, her face scared, then heard her coming quickly to the door.

'Hi.' Her face was pale and her hair scrambled.

Jack pushed his way inside, ignoring the other sleeping bodies. Someone muttered in their sleep.

Rachel was dressed in a T-shirt and pants and she hugged her arms across her chest.

'You sure you want to go, Rach?'

She nodded. 'We can't stay. Not now Adam . . .' She didn't finish the sentence but turned and quickly put on the rest of her clothes.

Jack said nothing about Tyler. As soon as Tyler discovered that some of his cash was missing, he'd be after Jack. How long would it be before he realised? A few hours? A day?

They had to move on. He knew he wouldn't be able to stay with her much longer anyway, knew his time was running out. And now it wasn't only Adam who would be looking for them.

'Yeah,' he said. 'We need to get away from Adam. Put some distance between us.'

Rachel frowned. 'The money's not going to go far.'

Jack shrugged. 'We'll find something.'

Fat chance.

Out loud, he said, 'We'll hitchhike. Just get far enough away. Then we'll decide what to do.'

She nodded.

'We'd better go now, Rach.'

'Yeah.' She looked behind her at the sleeping girls. 'Jack?'

'Yeah.'

She scrabbled around in her bag and handed him a pen and scrap of paper.

'What's this for?'

'Can you write a note for Yelena? Tell her thanks.'

'OK.'

She took it from him when he'd finished and squinted at it before carefully placing it on the chair next to Yelena's bunk.

Moments later, they were creeping out of the farm gates. A few people were up and about but no one looked curious. Rachel patted her backpack.

'She's a good mate, that Yelena,' she said. 'She gave me this backpack. Said it was old and she was getting a new one. And she wrote down her phone number for me. Said we must stay in touch.'

It was such a small act of kindness but for some reason it hit Jack hard. *There was a time*, he thought, *when I'd take kindness for granted. Something that happened every day.*

Last night he'd told Raffi he'd have to leave, letting him believe it was because of Tyler and the others. Raffi had told him he'd be welcome to keep sleeping on the floor in their already overcrowded van. When Jack had said it was better if he went, Raffi had pressed some food on him and written down his mobile number too.

They were only a few metres down the road when they heard a noise behind them.

'Oh no!' Rachel turned round, her face pinched and scared, but then she relaxed and started to laugh. 'I don't believe it. That bleeding dog!'

Jack stopped as the dog came bounding up to him. He stooped down and fondled its ears.

'I'm sorry, boy, you can't come with us.' He picked up a stick and flung it in the direction of the farm. 'Go on. Get off.'

Rachel was still laughing. 'See, I told you not to go making friends with it.'

The dog rushed after the stick, picked it up and then came straight back to Jack, dropping it at his feet, tail wagging in expectation. Jack patted him again and walked on.

'He'll get fed up and go back soon,' he said.

Rachel grinned. 'You're soft, you.'

Jack smiled. 'Not that soft,' he said. 'When we hitch a ride, he's on his own.'

At first there was little traffic on the road and Rachel became more and more nervous.

'Can't we get off the main road? We're easy to spot.'

Jack was as nervous as she was but he tried not to let it show.

'We need to be on the big road to get a lift,' he said.

At last, a lorry slowed down. The driver looked out of the window as they ran up to speak to him and frowned when he saw the dog beside Jack. 'That dog coming, too?'

'No, he's . . .' began Jack, but the dog had already leaped into the cab and refused to budge when Jack and Rachel tried to pull him out.

The lorry driver looked at them. 'Well, you can't leave him on the side of the road,' he said.

'He's not ours,' snapped Rachel.

'He is now,' said Jack suddenly, heaving himself up beside the dog. Rachel climbed in beside him.

'What the hell?' she whispered. But Jack didn't answer and, instead, he put his arm protectively round the dog and asked the driver where he was headed.

'I've got a delivery about fifty miles south of here,' he said. 'That suit you?'

'South?' chipped in Rachel. 'Is that towards London?'

'You're a long way from London, love.' And then, when she didn't answer, he added, 'You kids in some sort of trouble?'

'No,' said Jack quickly. 'We've been doing some fruit picking and we're on our way home.'

The lorry driver grunted, then he eased off the clutch and joined the traffic on the main road.

They'd been going for about half an hour when Jack happened to glance in the wing mirror and saw a car coming up the road behind them, going slowly. As it drew out to pass the lorry, Jack ducked his head and pushed Rachel down.

'Hey, give over,' she began, but Jack frowned at her and pointed to the car. Rachel slunk down further and didn't sit up again until the car was out of sight round the next bend.

'Was that Adam?' whispered Rachel.

Jack nodded.

The driver slid a glance across to them. 'What's going on? You kids being chased by someone? You're not in trouble with the police, are you?'

'No. Nothing like that,' said Jack.

But the lorry driver wouldn't let it go. He stared at Rachel. 'Hey, have you run away from home?'

'NO!' she shouted. 'How many times –'

Jack nudged her.

The driver shrugged and looked away. 'OK, OK, no need to shout. Just thought I'd seen you before somewhere.'

Jack glanced across at Rachel.

Seen her somewhere? How could he, unless . . . But no, surely no one had done that . . .

The rest of the journey passed mostly in uneasy silence and, an hour later, the lorry driver dropped them in the centre of a small town. By now it was mid-morning; it was market day and the town was full of jostling crowds.

It should be easy to stay hidden here, thought Jack.

'I'm busting for a wee,' said Rachel.

'You're always busting for a wee,' muttered Jack. He heaved his backpack over his shoulder. 'OK. We can go and get a coffee at that café and make a plan.'

The café wouldn't allow the dog inside so they had to tie him up out the front. He seemed quite happy and lapped from a bowl of water, then lay down in a patch of shade.

'OK,' said Jack, when Rachel joined him at the table. 'You want to go to London – and I want to . . . move on.'

She nodded towards the window. 'We'll never get there if we have to take that old fleabag with us.'

Jack looked at the dog. 'I like him,' he said stubbornly. 'If you want to split, I'll take him with me.'

She glared at him and then shook her head.

She couldn't keep her hands still and she began to trace a pattern in some spilled coffee on the surface of the table. 'I need you, Jack. I won't get nowhere on my own.' She hesitated. 'I know that now.'

Jack stared at her and suddenly she laughed.

'And you need me, an' all. Who else is going to worry about that cough of yours?'

'It's nothing.'

'Oh for Chrissake. Any idiot can see you're ill.'

Jack shook his head and smiled but she continued to stare at him.

'I've seen you before, ain't I?'

Jack shrugged. Would she remember? There'd been pictures in the papers at the time. Rachel couldn't read papers but she might have seen pictures.

'What happened to you, Jack?'

He dropped his eyes. 'You don't want to know.'

She was silent for a while, fiddling with her hair and taking noisy slurps from her coffee cup.

'D'you want to know what happened to me?'

'Go on, then.' Jack didn't raise his eyes.

Rachel continued to push her finger round and round, extending the wet patch of coffee further and further towards the centre of the table.

'I was put in care when I was four,' she said quietly.

Jack looked up. 'Four years old! Christ, Rach. What about . . . ? Wasn't there . . . ?'

'My mum was sick,' said Rachel, and her voice was so quiet that Jack had to lean towards her to hear.

'What sort of sick?'

Rachel sniffed. 'She loved me, Jack. I know she loved me. I can still remember . . . you know, bits and pieces. She hugged me and that. And . . . and she was always singing.'

'What happened to her?'

Rachel took a deep breath. 'She died, didn't she.'

'How? How did she die?'

Rachel's eyes filled with tears and she rubbed at them angrily with the back of her hand. Her reply was so quiet that Jack had to ask her to repeat it.

'Topped herself.'

Rachel's shoulders dropped and Jack saw that she was crying in earnest now. He put his hand out and caught hers, stopping the endless circular motion of the finger.

'I'm sorry.'

She nodded. 'It was years before I found out,' she said. 'When I was little I thought she put me away cos I was horrible.'

'Did she have . . . ?'

'I know what you're going to say. Yes, she had mental problems. That's why she did it, I guess.'

'And your dad?'

'Never knew who he was. I tried to find out once but . . .' She shrugged.

'And other relations? Your gran? Aunties and uncles?'

She shook her head. 'Didn't want to know.' She

sighed. 'Don't blame them; I was big trouble.'

'But surely not when you were little?'

'Can't really remember. They may have come to see me, but then I got difficult.'

They stayed there, Jack still holding her hand. He could feel that she was trembling.

'You're scared, aren't you, Rach? And it's not just Adam.'

She nodded. 'I'm scared I'm mental, like my mum.'

He continued to meet her eyes. 'Because of the voices?'

She nodded. 'I've never told no one about them before, not even the psych people they made me talk to.'

She shuddered suddenly. 'I don't know what'll happen to me, Jack. You're right; I'll never get a job. You've told me I'm stupid and I know I am. I can't read and I try to pretend I can.' She blushed and looked down at the table.

Jack grabbed hold of her other hand. 'Listen to me. You're not stupid. If you want to learn to read, I'll teach you.'

What am I saying? There's so little time!

'I'm too thick. I'll never learn.'

Jack grinned. 'Wanna bet?'

She sniffed again. 'I never got the hang of it at school. I'd sit looking at the letters but they didn't make no sense.'

They were silent for a while, then Jack peered out of the window. 'We've got to get further away, Rach. A good long way away from Adam, just in case . . .'

And Tyler will be after me, too.

She nodded. 'I know. That's why I want to go to London. He won't find me there, will he?'

Jack shook his head. 'No. Not now I've chucked the phone.'

Her head jerked up. 'You what? How dare you chuck out my phone! That was expensive, that was. And how we going to manage without it? We need a phone. Christ, Jack!'

'I had to get rid of it, Rach. He'd always be able to find us through the phone.'

'But that was mine! You had no right. What did you do with it?'

'Left it at the fruit farm.' He laughed suddenly. 'Perhaps Tyler's found it and he's getting the abuse from Adam.'

'Huh. Well, I'm not happy about it.'

'Well, you should be. Adam can't track us now and he's not likely to find us by driving up and down the road. We'll get another phone soon – a cheap one, pay as you go.'

The waitress was standing close by, staring at them. The place was filling up and they'd been sitting there ages, sharing a single mug of coffee.

'Have you finished?' she said, her hand stretching out for the mug.

Jack was about to nod, but Rachel cut in. 'No. We'll have another,' she said, scowling at the girl.

'Snotty cow,' she went on as the waitress retreated, muttering.

'She's only doing her job,' said Jack.

'I know her sort,' muttered Rachel. 'She thinks she's better than me.'

'Shut up and listen,' said Jack. 'If we want to get to London we've got to make a plan.'

'Well, we can't take that mongrel with us.'

Jack glanced out of the window and smiled. The dog was lying down asleep, its head on its forepaws. He took out his pad and made a quick sketch of him.

The waitress came back with the coffee and Jack thanked her. Rachel stared moodily down at the table.

'I'm gonna starve if I stay with you. I'd be better off with Adam.'

Jack didn't bother to look up. 'OK. Fine. Off you go.'

'You can give me my share of the money.'

'Fine,' repeated Jack. 'I expect there's a bus back from here.'

'He said he loved me.'

Jack sighed. 'If that's what you want . . .'

Rachel sniffed and rubbed her nose. 'I never had to worry about food or where to sleep and that.'

'Rach,' said Jack quietly. 'You *know* what they'll do to you if you go back.'

She nodded.

'And is that what you want?'

'I want food in my belly and a place to sleep. I don't wanna be scared all the time.'

'You'll be a whole heap more scared if you go back, Rach. They'll use you. They'll do your head in with drugs, then they'll throw you out when they're sick of you. And if you've got something on Adam . . .'

Rachel sniffed again. 'Yeah. I know I can't go back.' She paused. 'And you said you're no good for me, neither.'

'Maybe you're good for me.'

'Don't be daft!'

A plan was forming in his mind. He wouldn't tell her yet. He didn't even know if it would work.

He punched her lightly on the arm. 'Come on. It's you and me against the world, eh?'

She looked up at him and shook her head. 'You're nuts, you are.'

'You with me, then?'

'What do you mean?'

'No more going on about Adam?'

She made a face. 'You didn't ought to have chucked that phone.'

'Yes I should.'

When they walked out of the café, the dog stood up and stretched, wagging his tail at them.

'Stupid thing,' muttered Rachel.

Jack went up to him and untied him. He stroked his back. 'Don't take any notice of her,' he whispered into his wonky ear.

The three of them headed off, Rachel constantly looking over her shoulder.

'D'you think Adam's gonna keep looking for us?'

'I *told* you. He can't track us now.'

They'd soon left the town behind them and for the next hour they walked on, the sun shining down on them and the fields stretching on either side. Jack stopped often, sometimes coughing, sometimes just to rest. Rachel watched him. Once when they'd stopped, she pointed at the ripening wheat rippling in the light wind in the field beside the road.

'I don't like all these fields,' said Rachel. 'I feel safer with houses and that.'

Jack laughed. 'These fields grow stuff for you to eat, Rach.'

'Eh?'

Jack climbed the verge to the edge of the field, put his arm through the barbed-wire fence and plucked a stalk. He showed her the grains at the top. 'That's ground into flour to make bread and cakes and all sorts,' he said.

Rachel scowled at the stalk. 'You're joking me! How can those bobbly bits turn into bread?'

He started to explain but she was yawning.

'I'm dead knackered.'

Jack pointed over the hedge. 'There's a stream over there. We can sit down for a bit and let the dog have a drink too.'

They climbed a stile and walked down to the stream.

'What is it with you and fields?' said Rachel. 'We're always walking over sodding fields.'

Jack smiled. 'It's what they have in the country,' he said as he threw himself down on the bank. He undid the string from the dog's collar and it bounded straight into the water, drinking and splashing, then it rushed up the bank again and shook itself, sending droplets of water all over Rachel.

She swore, and Jack began laughing, quietly at first and then a full-bellied laugh coming up from his chest and turning into a cough.

Rachel turned to him. 'What are you laughing at?'

Then she, too, began to laugh.

'Bloody hell, who'd've believed it. You and me, eh?'

When he'd stopped laughing, Jack pulled his sketchpad out of his backpack. He wrote a few words on it and handed the pad to Rachel.

'What's this?'

'Your first lesson,' he said.

She pushed the pad back at him without looking at it.

'I can't.'

'You haven't even looked at it.'

She scowled. 'I don't need to.'

How can I reach her?

He thought for a bit and then began writing again, humming as he did so.

'How did it go, Rach? That song you were singing at the farm?'

'You're never trying to sing that! You're crap at it.'

'Tell me the words and I'll try again.'

She picked up a blade of grass and sat forward, concentrating, singing the words slowly, quietly.

Jack wrote them down. When she stopped singing, he handed her the pad again. 'There you are. The words of your song. Now you can see what they look like.'

She peered at the writing.

'Sing the words again,' said Jack. 'Slowly.'

'No!'

'Please. Just try.'

She sighed. 'I dunno why I stick with you.' But she started again, and as she sang the words, Jack took her finger and traced each word as she sang it.

'Now say them. And look at the words properly.'

She wriggled and her eyes slid away from the paper.

Jack began singing the words and she put her hands over her ears, laughing.

'Stop!'

But he went on singing.

'Bloody hell, Jack,' she said, but she started saying the words of the song and Jack stopped singing and, again, traced her finger along each word as she said it.

Again and again he made her do it until she jumped up.

'I'm sick of this. Let's go!'

Jack turned over the page and wrote three words.

'Recognise these?'

'What?'

She screwed up her eyes and looked at what he'd written.

Love.

Girl.

Passion.

'I've just been looking at those.'

Jack clapped his hands. 'Well done. Can you remember what they say?'

She repeated them back to him.

'There! That wasn't so bad, was it? End of first lesson.'

Suddenly she smiled. 'You sneaky sod!'

'You'll get there, Rach. Promise.'

'Huh!' she said.

Rachel

before

The first foster family wasn't too bad. They'd done loads of fostering before and the home said they were used to older kids. What they meant was older kids with issues. Big issues. I used to kick off a lot – still do – and they never shouted back. And I slammed a lot of doors too. And I couldn't take teasing.

One of the other foster kids, well, she knew how to needle me. She used to enjoy winding me up till I exploded. Then one day I went for her. Not just a bit of a flare up, this was a real rage. I can remember it; I really, really wanted to kill her and I swear to God that I would've done it if she hadn't screamed so loud that our foster dad and mum had come running. Even so, it took them an age to get me off her.

I'd never felt such rage welling up in me; when they talk about seeing red, well, that's just what I did. I was seeing red all right. When my foster parents calmed me down I couldn't believe what I'd done. I'd had a go at other kids in the home sometimes, but this was something else. She had deep scratches all down her face, all bleeding and I was holding chunks of her hair in my balled-up fists. I remember unclenching them and seeing all that mousy brown hair drift down to the floor.

Well, they had to send me back, then, didn't they? They said they were sad about it but I think they were just glad to get shot of me. They said they had no choice, that I was a danger to their other kids. What could I do? I went all sullen on them, refused to speak to them. Refused to say goodbye when the people came from the home to get me.

Then the usual rounds of talks with the social worker, the care-home people, the psych lady. She said something about rejection; that was the only thing that stuck in my mind. That word: rejection.

That's when the cutting began. Don't know how, or when, exactly. Think it was an accident first – or it may have been the voices telling me to do it. I remember seeing the blood seeping from the cut in my arm, watching it dribble into my hand and then drip onto the floor of the bathroom.

No one noticed at the home. No one cared. I mostly did it where it didn't show.

Drip, drip. The tension pouring out of me when it got unbearable. Even the psych lady never asked me whether I cut myself. She asked every other damn question, and if I refused to answer or showed signs of kicking off she just gave up.

They didn't try another foster home for a long time.

Chapter 7

Jack got to his feet, called the dog and attached the piece of string round its neck.

'You got a name for that fleabag, then?'

Jack patted the dog's head. 'Jasper,' he said, without hesitation.

Why did I say that?

'That's a poncy name for a dog!'

Jack shrugged.

They got back to the road and started walking again but there was little traffic. A tractor passed them, and a huge combine harvester and a Land Rover. Although they got some curious glances, no one stopped for them.

'We should go back to the big road,' said Rachel.

Jack shook his head. 'Not after that scare this morning. We can't risk it.'

'Hell, Jack, he's not going to spend the whole day

driving up and down that effing road looking for us.'

'OK. Tomorrow – we'll go back on it tomorrow.'

It wasn't the threat of Adam or Tyler. He was pretty sure they were far enough away by now, but Jack didn't want to leave the familiarity of the fields and the small winding road, the trees and the sound of birdsong, reminding him of when he and his mum . . . when they'd been happy, when life had been good.

His mind drifted. Back to his twin sisters. Six years old when he'd left home. They must have asked about him. What had his mum told them? He missed them with a physical ache. Whenever he saw kids playing, larking around, shouting, chasing each other, he thought of them. OK, a lot of the time they were a pain, but there were good moments too. He used to read to them, one each side of him, snuggled up on the big sofa in the lounge, and they'd look up at him, wide eyed, their thumbs in their mouths. He could still feel the warmth of their little bodies either side of him.

'I dunno why I fall in with everything you say,' muttered Rachel.

Jack snapped back to the present. 'What?'

'Hey, earth to Jack. What planet are you on?'

'Sorry. What did you say?'

'I said, I dunno why I always give in. Do what you want.'

'You got a better idea, then?'

'Yeah,' she said. 'Why don't we get a train to London?'

'Where from?'

'I dunno. Next town?' She looked at the dog. 'We'd have to get rid of him, though.'

Jack shook his head and fondled the dog's ears. 'He's coming with us.'

'For Chrissake, Jack.'

Jack turned to face her. His eyes were angry but when he spoke, his voice was soft. 'He chose us and he's loyal. I'm not letting him down.'

'He's only a bleeding *dog*!'

'You don't understand, do you?'

'No.'

Jack turned away so he didn't say something he'd regret.

Count to ten, he told himself as he thought back to that other Jasper. The dog he'd lost. Although he hadn't run off, hadn't got lost, had he?

Rachel sighed. 'We got any more to eat – for later?'

He didn't answer. He was beginning to feel it, that familiar feeling of being pulled away. He never had any warning it was about to happen. Damn! He was going to have to leave her – now, before she was safe. He should have left her at the farm where she had friends; perhaps if he'd gone then, she would have stood up to Adam, been protected by Raffi and Yelena.

God, what a mess. He'd failed her just as he'd failed

his mum. This was his last chance and he'd never be rid of the guilt now, never be able to move on.

'Hey, did you hear me?' said Rachel. 'We got any more to eat? And where are we going to sleep?'

Still Jack didn't answer. He couldn't. The lethargy was overwhelming him – the prelude, the build up.

Don't let it happen. Not now! Just a little more time.

He forced himself to go on walking, needing all his energy to put one foot in front of the other but as he looked down the road, his vision started to blur and the hedges came closer and then receded. He started to stagger, lurching from side to side.

Oh God.

And then he was on the ground.

He was safe again, curled up in his bed at home. The sound of his mum humming to the music on the radio as she cooked breakfast; the tree outside his window in full blossom, its scent drifting into his nostrils combining with the smell of bacon frying. The family together. Safe.

As soon as he'd collapsed, the dog had gone to him, licking his face, pawing at his chest. Rachel was beside him.

'What you doing, Jack?' She knelt down, yanked at his arm. 'What the hell's the matter?'

No response.

'Bleeding hell, Jack, don't play silly buggers with me.' She shook him, but some instinct told her it would do no good. His face was white, his body inert.

'Stop it, Jack. This isn't funny.' She shook him again, but less violently this time.

She sat back on her heels and started to cry. 'Don't get sick, Jack. Please don't get sick. I need you.'

She stared around her. No one about. Not a bleeding soul. If only they'd had the phone.

Jack groaned.

He was still alive! Relief flooded through her. She put her hand out to touch his head, push the matted hair out of his eyes.

'Get up, for Chrissake.'

The dog pushed its muzzle into the crook of her elbow. She didn't push it away.

For a few minutes, Jack drifted in and out of consciousness. He heard moaning but didn't associate the sound with himself. He wanted to hold on to the vision of the old house, of his mum and the twins, but they faded as he came back and was staring up into another face, another pair of eyes.

'Mum?' he muttered, but he knew it wasn't. As his vision cleared, he saw Rachel's face in front of him, scared, tears running down her cheeks.

'Jack,' she yelled at him. 'You half scared me to death. What happened?'

He tried to sit up but fell back, exhausted, his head spinning.

'I can't go on,' he whispered. 'It's . . .'

'Thank God you've come back. I thought you were dying, you daft bugger.'

He muttered something but she didn't hear him.

Rachel stared at him, chewing her nails. 'You need a doctor,' she said at last.

He shook his head – and immediately regretted it, the nausea coming in waves.

'Jack.'

Slowly, he sat up and put his head between his knees.

'No doctor,' he muttered.

'Why?'

He didn't answer.

She slid down to sit beside him, fiddling with her hair.

'Records,' she said. 'They got records and stuff. Is that why you don't want to see a doctor?'

'Yes.'

Let her think that.

She looked at him, frowning. 'It's not just Adam who's after you, then? You're on the run, aren't you?

'Yep.' It was easier to lie, though he supposed it was half true.

'Tell me about it?'

'Not now.'

'What shall I do, Jack? You can't stay here, lying in the road.'

He closed his eyes and lay back.

Rachel looked about her. Nothing. Nothing but flowers and grass and fields. She got to her feet and paced up and down, wanting to run away from it all, get the hell out, take no responsibility. It was what she'd always done. Then she looked down at Jack. He'd got her here, into the sodding countryside, hadn't he? It was his fault.

'What shall I do?' She shouted the question this time, hands on hips, looking down at him.

'Get me out of sight,' he gasped.

'What?'

'Hide me. Here,' he said, putting out an arm. 'Help me up.'

She sighed and yanked at his arm. Very slowly, he got to his feet, hanging on to her, leaning on her heavily, swaying. Together they shuffled to a gap in the hedge and Jack sat down behind it. His breath was short and Rachel could see the beads of sweat on his forehead. The dog lay down beside him.

'I just need to rest up a bit,' said Jack. 'Go and look for a barn or something. Somewhere we can stay the night.'

'Where am I going to find a bleeding barn?' she muttered.

'Go on, Rach. You can do it.'

She stood, uncertain, frowning.

Jack tugged at her hand. 'Please.'

She moved away slowly. 'All right, all right.'

She'd only walked a few metres when she turned round.

'Don't you run off when I'm gone.'

Jack managed a faint smile. He had no control, now. Would he be able to stay until she came back? If he was gone by then he'd just be another bloke in her life who'd failed her.

Rachel walked a little way down the road, then she heard the sound of a car approaching and she darted behind a hedge. Crouching there, she watched it pass. Not Adam, thank God. Perhaps she should have tried to stop it.

I can't do this on my own.

You don't have to.

A voice was in her head but it was the soft voice. The good one. By itself, this time, just for a moment, not muddled up with all the other shouting, gabbling ones.

She stayed very still, listening.

Then the tune, the familiar tune. Quietly at first, then more strongly, the tune that always made her cry, bringing back that faint, faint memory. Only the memory was stronger than it had been in the past, of a hand holding hers, guiding her as she walked on something – something high. What was it? A wall? It was at the edge of her memory but still out of reach.

'Help me,' whispered Rachel.

A picture formed in her mind. She tried to focus. What had Jack said – a barn? But the picture didn't look like a barn. She wasn't even sure what a barn looked like, anyway. But it was a building – and more words were coming into her head. *Not far . . . up the path to some trees.*

But the gentle voice was fading and the others, the jabbering horrible ones were taking over.

Stay – please stay!

Only Rachel's thoughts, but she knew they were heard.

Just for a moment, the picture solidified in front of her eyes, but then it was gone again and there was nothing. Just a thorny hedge and some stinging nettles.

Rachel swore. She'd been listening so carefully to the voice that she'd not felt the nettles. Now they really hurt. She stumbled out onto the road again, scratching at the bumps coming up in the gap between her jeans and her trainers.

'I hate the country,' she said out loud, ducking as a black and white bird swooped low over her head.

She walked on and rounded a corner. No sign of a building.

She stopped and picked off a thorn that had stuck

in her jacket; what was she like, in these horrible clothes Jack had given her – and these gross trainers? They didn't fit properly and they rubbed her feet. And her hair was filthy too. She'd kill for a shower. She rubbed at her eyes, puffy with crying. She'd never felt so alone.

You're not alone.

The voice again. Soothing; under the others, but clear. She sniffed.

Not much further. Keep going.

Rachel started walking again. What choice did she have? Jack was sick. She had to get him some place where he could rest.

She kept staring around her but she couldn't see anything that looked like a barn or a shed. But then, gradually, her sight began to blur and the fields and the hedges began to fade away. She could no longer see clearly in front of her. She rubbed her eyes again and she hesitated, unwilling to go on.

Then suddenly everything seemed normal again, and she saw it – a small path winding up between the trees on her right. But it hadn't been there before. She could swear it hadn't been there before.

This is doing my head in.

Go on!

That damned voice again.

She stepped off the road and onto the path. It

wound steeply up and she puffed and panted as she climbed, sometimes having to grab onto branches of young trees for support. As she climbed higher, the trees became more tightly packed on either side of the path and only faint beams of sunlight filtered through. Rachel shivered.

'There's nothing here,' she said aloud.

Look up.

She stopped and looked up. She screwed up her eyes and stared.

She could swear it hadn't been there a moment before. She would have seen it. A wooden building, in a clearing a little way in from the path. How had she missed it? Cautiously, she fought her way through the trees and undergrowth towards it.

At last she could stand up straight on the level ground. She wiped her muddy hands on her jeans and walked up to the hut, peering in through a window at the side.

Blankets, food, a table.

The door will be locked. I won't be able to get in.

But there was no bolt and she lifted the latch on the door and pushed inside.

It was clean and there were tins of food, matches, a camping stove, even a first-aid box. It must belong to someone.

You can stay here.

The voice was so close that Rachel whipped round,

but there was nothing. Just the smell of the rotting leaves on the ground beneath the trees.

Is this real?

Believe it.

Rachel rubbed her eyes and shook her head.

'Will it be here when I come back with Jack?'

Believe it.

She stamped her foot and turned round quickly. No one. Nothing. She put her hands either side of her head and shook it from side to side.

What's wrong with me? Am I seeing things that aren't even there now?

No answer. She turned her back on the hut and waited. She shut her eyes and then after a few seconds opened them again and turned round quickly.

It was still there. And it looked solid enough.

OK. OK. I'll bring him here.

She ran down the path, slipping, sliding, scared. Was it real? Was the path real? It seemed real enough, the bushes catching at her arms, the soil and leaf mould under her feet squelchy and creeping into her trainers.

She crashed out from the path onto the road and stood there, bent over to ease the stitch in her side. Her head was buzzing, snatches of songs colliding together, words, pictures, voices louder and louder. It had never been this bad before.

When she'd got her breath, she started running

back up the road, the way she'd come, round the bend. She looked about her. Damn it, every field and hedge looked the same to her. She went on running, conscious of her feet in the oversized trainers, slap-slapping on the tarmac. Surely it wasn't this far away, was it?

'Jack!' she shouted.

No answer.

'Jack,' she yelled, louder this time.

There was a rustling sound behind her and she spun round. He was on all fours, crawling back through the hedge. She put her hands on her hips.

'Why didn't you answer? Didn't you hear me?'

He said nothing, but rose shakily to his feet and started to brush the leaves and twigs off his clothes. His face was still very pale and although he was looking at her, his eyes didn't seem to focus.

'Where's yer pack?'

He jerked his thumb at the hedge. 'Over there.' His voice was strange, hoarse.

'What, so I've got to fetch it for you, have I? I'm your bleeding servant now, am I?'

He didn't react, so she pushed through the hedge and came back lugging it behind her.

'It weighs a bleeding ton.'

'Tell me about it,' muttered Jack.

She came close to him. 'I think I've found somewhere,' she said.

He blinked and frowned as if he was trying to understand her.

'I found a place to stay,' she said.

He was still not focusing on her.

'You going to say thanks?'

He didn't say anything and she blew out her lips and then bent down to scratch her itching legs.

'Come on, then, I'll show you.'

'I can't walk far.'

'It's not far.'

Is it far? she thought. *I don't know. I don't even know if it will still be there. Please let it still be there.*

She took his hand then, and he let her lead him, very slowly, along the road and round the bend, the dog trotting behind them. She peered into the trees.

Nothing. No path.

She stopped and closed her eyes, trying to imagine the path in her head, and the hut in the clearing. Very slowly, a picture came into her mind and she opened her eyes again. She let out a sigh.

'There,' she said, pointing towards the path.

Jack frowned. 'I can't see anything.'

'Believe me, it's there. Come on.'

'I can't . . .'

'Follow me. I'll show you.'

'Rach, is this some stupid trick?'

'No. Come on.'

Can he see it? Will he be able to see the hut too?

They made very slow progress up the steep track, the dog constantly at their heels. Rachel kept slipping as she climbed, the heavy backpack unbalancing her as she dragged Jack upwards. They kept having to stop so that Jack could stoop over and stop the dizziness in his head and take shallow breaths. Once he had a coughing fit and Rachel thought the hacking noise would never stop.

Then, at last, they were at the clearing.

'See?' said Rachel.

Jack raised his head and stared. 'Is it real?'

'Why do you say that?'

'I dunno. I just feel . . . weird. Like, like I'm in a sort of dream. My head's all fuzzy.'

'You blacked out, Jack. You're sick. We can rest up here for a bit. Decide what to do next. You can get better.'

He didn't reply.

Jack

before

Someone had persuaded Mum to try an online dating site and that's where she'd met Kevin. It took her ages to agree to meet up with him but when they did, she'd told me that they'd really clicked. They had so much in common. And at first I liked him. He was a good-looking, sporty guy but he didn't try to replace Dad or anything – and Mum seemed really happy.

They were small things at first: the hand on my shoulder that squeezed just a bit too hard, the time when I saw him kick the dog – the first Jasper.

And then Jasper disappeared.

Kevin was all sympathy. 'He must have run off,' he said. 'It happens.'

'We'll get another dog,' Mum promised. But I didn't want another dog. I didn't want the twins' hearts broken again – or mine.

Then there were his grand plans.

'Kevin's trying to set up this company,' Mum said. 'I'm going to help him.'

All optimism and excitement at first, then the doubts.

'Nothing to worry about. It's a long-term investment.'

'It'll take time to see a return.'

Then, 'We're going to sell the house, move somewhere cheaper.' Mum wouldn't meet my eyes when she told me and she wouldn't discuss it with me when we packed up and moved to the city up north where Kevin swore he'd be able to get work, where he said he had contacts, where everything would be all right. All right for Kevin, maybe, but not for me, changing schools, thrown suddenly into a big inner-city comp.

It was ages before I found out the truth. How Kevin had bled us dry – of her money, Dad's money.

And the rows. Mum wasn't one to confront issues but when no job materialised, when it became obvious that Kevin wasn't even trying to find work but was just hanging around bars in the city, she tried to reason with him, and that was when his dark side came out. When the violence started.

At first, she had hidden it well, wearing long-sleeved tops and making up stories about falling over or bumping into things. But then one day I saw the bruises on her arms. Long, finger-shaped bruises.

Chapter 8

Once they were inside, the tune in her head was louder. Rachel glanced at Jack, wondered if he could hear it.

Jack stared around. 'What is this place?'

Rachel shrugged. 'Don't ask me. How should I know? But it's OK, isn't it? There's food and blankets and stuff.'

Jack nodded. He couldn't fight it any more. Rachel spread out the blankets and he lay down and closed his eyes. Jasper was soon beside him, his rough-coated body right up against Jack's, lending him warmth.

Rachel stood looking at them both for a while, the tune still playing in her head – and the voice was there, too, but it was just the gentle one now, not the annoying, bossy, shouting ones. She looked at all the tins stacked up on the shelves but she couldn't read the labels. She picked one up and recognised the picture on the front. Baked beans. Great. She pulled the tab and peeled off the top, sniffing the familiar smell. Then she found a saucepan and tipped them in. It took her a while to light the stove and adjust the flame but at last she managed to heat up the beans.

'Here, Jack. I've done some cooking!'

Jack opened his eyes and smiled at her, then he went back to sleep.

For the first time since they'd left the shopping mall, Rachel felt safe. She knew that Adam wouldn't find them here. She looked down at Jack, snoring lightly now, his face relaxed.

He feels safe too.

Rachel ate all the baked beans, as she squatted on the floor beside Jack. The dog raised his head and whined.

'What's up with you, you mangey mutt?'

He whined again.

'I suppose you're hungry.'

What do dogs eat? What did Jack feed it?

She looked around at their supplies and saw a tin with meat chunks on the front. Carefully, she opened it up and spooned some out for the dog. He gulped it down in one and then looked up hopefully. She gave him a bit more and he wagged his tail at her. She sniffed at the meat. It smelled good so she had some too. Then she found some bottled water and had a drink, pouring some into another saucepan for Jasper. The dog lapped it up and then settled down again, its body pressed against Jack's.

It was nearly evening and the sun was beginning to go down behind the trees that surrounded the hut. Rachel saw a lantern but she couldn't work out how to light it. As Jack continued to sleep, she took his torch out of his backpack and examined all the tins. She started with the ones she recognised: baked beans, tuna, soups – they all had pictures on them. She looked at the letters and tried to memorise them, mouthing them out.

I should be scared, she thought. *It's getting dark and we're in the middle of trees and there's birds and animals and stuff, but I'm not. And I'm not scared someone's going to find us here, cos I know they won't.*

The tune, which had only been a background noise in her head, got gradually louder.

Outside the hut she heard some small rustling noises and she shivered.

Only animals. Nothing to be afraid of.

Rachel took another of the blankets and wrapped it round herself before lying down the other side of the dog so that it was between her and Jack. Tentatively, she put out a hand to stroke its rough fur. Jasper turned his head towards her and licked her face.

'Stupid thing,' said Rachel, but she didn't turn away from him.

It was late afternoon when Jack woke. He looked around him, dazed, confused, not knowing where he was at first. Then he saw Rachel stirring something in a saucepan, which she'd put on top of a camping stove.

He propped himself up on one elbow.

''Bout time too,' said Rachel, not looking up from her task. 'Here, have some food.'

She scooped a mass of something white and sticky onto a plate and handed it to him.

'What's this?'

'Dunno. But it isn't half bad. Taste it.'

She handed him a spoon.

Jack sniffed. 'It's rice pudding!'

'Eh?'

Slowly, Jack began to eat. Rachel stared at him.

'You feeling better?' she said at last.

He nodded as he finished the rice pudding, scraping the last of it off the plate with the spoon. 'How did we get here?' he asked.

Rachel looked away. 'I found it, didn't I?'

'OK,' he said slowly.

'What?' she asked.

He shrugged. 'Nothing. It's just . . . I dunno, a bit weird.'

She folded her arms. 'What's weird?'

'Finding it here. And with all this stuff in it. It's as if . . .'

'As if what?'

'Oh, forget it. My head's still buzzing. Take no notice.'

'No one can find us here,' said Rachel.

'Unless the people who stocked this place come back,' said Jack.

'They won't. Not now.'

'How can you be so sure?'

Rachel didn't answer his question. Instead she sat down beside him and started eating some biscuits she'd found.

'OK,' she said, through a mouthful. 'Now you can tell me something.'

Jack tensed. 'What?'

'What's wrong with you, Jack? And don't keep saying you've just got a cough. I'm not stupid.'

How much should he tell her?

'OK,' he said, after a pause. 'I've got a . . . You're right, there is something wrong with me – with my chest – but it's OK so long as I don't . . .'

'So long as you don't rush about or sleep rough or eat rubbish food, is that it?'

He smiled. 'Something like that.'

'So you haven't been doing yourself any favours since you've been on the run.'

Jack sat up abruptly. 'Who said I was on the run?'

'You did. Remember? You told me someone else was after you – not just Adam.'

Jack frowned. 'I did?'

She nodded and licked her plate clean.

The silence lay heavily between them and suddenly the birdsong from the trees and the snores from Jasper seemed unbearably loud. Then, after a while, Rachel turned to look at him.

'This place . . .' she began. 'I don't know how . . . It's really weird, isn't it? And I feel safe here. We're safe, aren't we, Jack?'

He nodded. 'For the moment,' he said quietly.

The pull he'd felt earlier wasn't so strong now. Had he been given a bit more time? He'd already been too long, he knew that. And it was Rachel who had found the place, not him. Who had directed her? How? How had she known?

Jack got up and started to look round the hut, picking up tins of food and examining them, opening the drawers in the table and taking out the two sets of cutlery – spoons, knives, forks. He opened the first-aid box and looked inside.

'It's like it's only just been put here,' he said, frowning. 'Nothing's rusty or damp.' He found a roll of black bin bags and tore one off. 'Here, we'll use this for rubbish,' he said, tossing the empty tins into it. He saw a spade propped up in the corner. He pointed at it. 'We can use that when we need the toilet,' he said.

'What!'

'Dig a hole, do a poo,' he said.

'Yuk. No way!'

'You got a better suggestion?'

She didn't answer. She was fingering her clothes. 'I look a mess. I need a shower and clean stuff.'

'We'll get some, Rach, when we move on.'

'And my feet are wrecked.'

'Yeah. I know.'

She smiled at him suddenly. 'You're looking out for me, right?'

He shrugged. 'You're looking out for me too.'

He sat down beside her, their backs against the wooden wall of the hut. Rachel was fingering the chain at her neck.

'You're always doing that,' Jack said.

'What?'

'Touching that necklace.'

She drew it out from under her T-shirt and showed it to him.

He took the silver chain between his finger and thumb. At its end hung a heart-shaped locket.

Rachel smiled. 'It was my mum's.'

'Yeah? How d'you know?'

'They told me she put it round my neck before she . . .' Rachel looked away. 'Anyway, they let me keep it at the home. I wear it all the time.'

'What's in the locket part?'

Rachel put her bitten nails to the clasp and gently opened it. Inside was a tiny, faded photo of a young woman with a baby.

Jack peered at it. 'That you and your mum?'

'I think so.'

Rachel held it up close to her eyes. The photo was so faded she could no longer make out the features clearly. She snapped it shut and let the locket drop under her T-shirt again.

'You got anything from your family, Jack?'

'Not now.' He turned away.

'D'you miss them?'

'Doesn't matter. I can't go back.'

'Why not? What happened?'

He looked down at the floor of the hut, but he was hearing again the sound of the footsteps on the stairs – heavy, deliberate – coming up to his room.

He shook his head. There was no way he could explain.

'Who's after you?'

He looked her in the eyes, then said, 'I'm a missing person.'

'What, like on posters and stuff?'

He smiled. 'Sort of.'

'Who's looking for you – the police?'

'Not exactly.'

It was winter when he'd left – cold, with a biting wind. That was when he got ill, sleeping rough in bad weather.

'You don't have to tell me.'

Rachel's voice interrupted his thoughts. He swallowed. He couldn't tell her. He couldn't tell anyone.

'I miss him,' said Rachel suddenly.

'Who?'

'Adam,' she said quietly.

'Oh, Rach!'

'Yeah, I know. I know he's bad an' that. But no one's ever bin that nice to me before.' She nudged him, 'Except you, I s'pose.'

Jack put out a hand and held hers. They sat together for a moment and then Jack rose unsteadily to his feet. 'I'd better take the dog out,' he said.

'Be careful. Don't let anyone see you.'

'They won't.' He said it with complete confidence.

Jack called to Jasper and the dog rose reluctantly, stretched and yawned, then trotted over to Jack who opened the door of the hut and peered out.

Once outside, he looked around him. He loved the quietness, the smell of leaf mould and the chatter of the birds. He walked on the even ground for a bit beyond the hut, but then it petered out and he either had to climb up the hill or down. Up, he decided.

Slowly. Take it slowly.

Jasper bounded up and down between the trees, snuffling and barking, chasing leaves and occasionally picking up a stick and bringing it back to Jack. Jack climbed a little higher and then stopped to catch his breath. And then again, a bit higher. It took him a long time but at last he was right at the top of the path. The trees were less dense here and he followed the path until he came to a gate looking over fields and down into the valley.

The view took his breath away. Here it was all grassland, none of the endless fields of ripe wheat they'd passed on the road. Here there were rolling hills, pastures, cows. It was beautiful. His sketchpad and pencil were in the pocket of his jacket and he took them out.

He climbed over the gate and sat with his back against it, drawing. He wasn't aware of time, just of the shapes of the hills, the shadows from the clouds on the hillside, a tiny church spire in the far distance. Jasper tired of chasing and sniffing and came to lie down beside him.

It was the changing sky that brought him back to earth – that and the sudden warning pulse of pain in his head. The sun had gone in and it was overcast now, the clouds rolling in from the west. It was going to rain. He'd been so absorbed that he'd hardly noticed time passing, or that the tightening in his chest had got worse.

Quickly he got to his feet and skidded down the path back to the hut, Jasper at his heels. By the time he'd reached the door, he was out of breath and sweating.

'Sorry, Rach. I was –' He looked round the hut. 'Rachel?'

It was empty.

Idiot! He'd been gone too long. Why couldn't she trust him, know he'd come back? Had she gone looking for him?

He took some deep breaths. He was in a safe, calming place. Once outside, it would be harder to control the pain. He fought the overwhelming urge to stay there and hope she'd come back, that she would find it again, but he knew she might not.

Reluctantly, he called Jasper, turned for the door and went out. Which way would she go?

He didn't want to climb up the steep hill again so he struck off through the trees. The sun was sinking fast and the leaf canopy above him didn't let in much light. Jasper bounded ahead of him, sniffing at the ground, his tail wagging. Jack watched him and smiled.

How good it would be to be able to live each moment as it came, not to worry about the past – or the future.

Jack stopped and stood still, listening. The birds were settling in the trees but there was no other sound.

'Rachel!' He called out as loudly as he could, then bent over with a fit of coughing.

Nothing. Except that Jasper came crashing back through the trees at the sound of his voice. Jack put out his hand and stroked the rough head.

'Find her, boy,' he said quietly. 'You can find her.'

Jasper set off again, nose to the ground. It was getting darker all the time but Jasper's pale fur stood out in the gloom. Jack followed the dog, stumbling after him, sometimes catching his foot in undergrowth and pitching forward onto all fours, but all the time keeping his eyes on the dog as it leaped effortlessly over fallen logs, its limbs perfectly coordinated.

Such a silent creature. Jack had never heard it bark. But then it was a lurcher, a gypsy dog bred for generations to hunt silently, to poach in woods, to get food for the pot.

At least an hour must have passed and still they'd not found her. Jack's chest was bursting with pain and he was beginning to feel faint again. He knew he had to get back to the safety of the hut. He called Jasper to him and they started to retrace their steps.

But it was darker still and, although Jack could swear

he was going back the way he had come, everything looked unfamiliar.

It's the dark, he told himself. *It all looks different in the dark.*

But after a while he had to admit that he was lost. Was the hut even there any more? Could he find it without Rachel?

He sat down on the damp, leafy ground and hugged his knees to him.

Think! Get your head straight. You have to find the hut. You're no good to her if you're not strong.

He needed the injection of calm to keep going on. He knew it wouldn't last but he'd survive as long as she needed him and as long as she was near – and they were safe. That's how it worked. He was beginning to understand that now. It had never been like this before. Before he'd only been there at the critical moment, only needed to be there for that. He'd never had to stay with the mark, be on the run with the mark. All this was new territory. At the hut he'd felt well, had felt he could stay longer, but it had been an illusion. He raised his head again, feeling weaker and dizzier. His time was running out. Damn it. Now the dog had disappeared too.

Jack struggled to his feet, keeping his head down to try to clear it.

'Jasper!' he called faintly.

Nothing.

Oh God. I've blown it this time. I can't leave her now, alone in the woods, in the countryside where she's unhappy and scared. She's a city girl, she doesn't understand life out here – it's so alien to her.

He stumbled on, one foot in front of the other, really slowly now, but he had no idea whether he was going in the right direction.

Was this the clearing? It all looked different in the dark. And there was no hut.

He stood completely still as the minutes ticked by, listening. Then an owl hooted, quite close, and he jumped, his heart racing.

And then, when he knew he was lost, when despair crept over him like a second skin, he heard it.

A bark.

Jack jerked his head up quickly and turned in the direction of the noise. Was that Jasper? But the dog had never barked before. He strained peering into the darkness, trying to work out exactly where it was coming from.

Then it came again, a bit closer this time. Was the dog coming towards him? Could Jasper smell him?

Then the sound of twigs breaking underfoot. That couldn't be the dog – it was too light to break anything. Was it another dog? A dog with a human? Jack tensed himself against a tree. He couldn't run. He could hardly move. He shut his eyes and waited.

The noise was nearer now – the panting of a dog and footsteps after it, crashing through the undergrowth. Jack closed his eyes.

And then they were upon him. First Jasper, jumping up, his paws on Jack's chest, reaching out with his tongue to lick Jack's face. Jack stumbled backwards and fell, landing on his hand as he put it out to save himself.

'Ow!'

And then she was there, too, breathless.

'Where did you go?' she yelled at him, and her voice echoed round the wood. And then, before he had time to answer, she was on the ground beside him, sobbing and pummelling his chest, her incoherent words coming out in rushes.

'I could've died! Why didn't you come back? There was animals and stuff and it was getting dark.'

Painfully, Jack sat up. 'I'm sorry, Rach,' he said quietly. 'I'm so sorry.'

Eventually she stopped crying and rubbed her eyes.

'I can't see nothing. Where's the bleeding hut?'

And suddenly it came to him. The hut would come back, but they had to be together. The place of safety wouldn't be real, not if he wasn't with her.

He stood up slowly and brushed the leaves and twigs off his jeans. Then he emptied his mind, closed his ears to Rachel's ranting, the dogs nudges, and focused. Imagined that solid little hut with its corrugated iron roof and all the supplies inside. Imagined himself going up to the door again and lifting the latch.

He opened his eyes and stared towards the patch of even ground. Sure enough, there was an outline of something. Something that hadn't been there a few moments ago. Even in the dark he could sense the bulk of it.

'Over there,' he said confidently, and started walking towards it.

Rachel

before

There was another foster family after that. I was scared. I didn't like the home much but you knew where you were there. The family were OK, I s'pose. But I knew they were just doing it for the money. And they were dead boring. That's when I started bunking off. Wandering round the streets, hooking up with gangs and that. That's when I started drinking too.

I knew my life was pointless. Is that how my mum felt when she topped herself? But she'd had me, hadn't she? I felt so angry with her. Why did she leave me like that? Then I'd hold on to the chain to stop the thoughts clogging my brain. She'd given me that. And she'd bothered to put the photo in the locket thing.

It was going to happen, I knew it would. I just lived day to day, pretending to go to school but wandering the streets. I was dead clever at looking out for the cops but they picked me up in the end. Then the usual boring rounds of interviews, assessments and meetings. I zoned out. What did it matter? What did anything matter? I swore to myself that I'd never let on about the voices. They were private. All these people knew everything there was to know about me – or they thought they did – but they didn't know about my voices and I wasn't ever going to tell them.

Chapter 9

They spent several days and nights in the hut, cocooned in silence and safety, with enough to drink and eat. It was a while before they realised that everything inside the hut was old.

Rachel held up some boxes and tins for Jack to see, laughing and pointing. 'Look at the pictures on this box, Jack, the kid here's wearing a really old-fashioned dress.'

Jack shrugged. 'So?' he said. 'It's an old box.'

'Yeah. But not *old* old. They're not, like, rusty or mouldy. They're in good nick.'

He didn't answer. She went on. 'It's as if they've been here for years waiting for us.'

What a weird thing to say.

'D'you think I'm daft?'

'No,' he said slowly. 'I know what you mean. The whole place is in a sort of time warp.'

There. He'd said it. Would she realise?

She frowned at him, not understanding.

'Anyway,' he said. 'I'm not knocking it. It's been good here, hasn't it?'

She nodded. 'You look better, Jack.'

It was true. His cough had gone, his colour had returned. He was strong again. It was almost time to move on but he was reluctant, knowing what lay ahead, knowing that once they were out in the real world, he'd have no protection and he'd have to leave her.

Rachel began to be restless too. 'It's funny,' she said. 'I feel happy here even though it's in the middle of all these trees.'

He'd had time to go on with her reading lessons. She'd been reluctant at first, putting it off, pretending she had to do something, darting outside, but in the end she'd settled down with him – and his sketchpad.

They established a routine. They'd wake, find something to eat, then settle down for an hour together. She would sing a song, he would write down the words, she would learn them and then painstakingly trace over them with her finger and finally write them herself.

He drew for her too. Everything that surrounded them: the birds, the trees, the dog, the hut, their clothes, the door, the window, the stove, and she would learn the words in the same way. Then she would think of a word – sometimes a word she used a lot, sometimes a word plucked randomly from her past. Occasionally this would upset her as it brought flashbacks.

One day, as they were sitting side by side, Jack said, 'What about the words in your head, Rach? Can you tell me what they are?'

'The voices aren't there all the time,' she said.

'When do they come most?'

She frowned and scratched her ear. 'When I'm stressed,' she said quietly.

'What do they tell you to do when you're stressed?'

She looked down at the floor. 'Bad things.'

'Like?'

'I dunno. To hit someone, to steal from the shops, to swear at someone, to shout.'

'Are there any good voices?'

She nodded. 'Sometimes.'

'Like when?'

'There's the one that's been coming a bit here.'

'What, while we've been in the hut?'

'Yeah.'

'And what does the good voice tell you to do?'

She got up abruptly and walked over to the door. 'Forget it; you wouldn't understand. No one can understand if they don't hear them.'

'OK,' he said, putting away the sketchpad and stretching his arms above his head. 'D'you feel like moving on again?'

She stopped, her hand on the latch of the door.

'To London?'

'If that's where you want to go.'

She turned then and gave him a grin. 'No one's going to come looking for me there.'

Jack thought of the posters they'd had of him. They'd be after her too, surely, wherever she went. The whole machinery of the welfare services. Police, social services, the care home. Or would they? Had she disappeared so often that the authorities had lost interest?

No,' he agreed. 'You'll be safe there.'

And suddenly he knew where he could take her to make sure she was safe. Safe and well cared for.

They were quiet for a moment, then Rachel started to fiddle with her hair. 'It's funny. Since we've been here I haven't needed a fix. And I don't feel stressy. It's weird.'

'What about the cutting?'

Rachel's head shot up. 'What?'

'You heard.'

She looked down at the floor. 'You got second sight or something?'

'I've seen the scars, Rach.'

She continued to look down. 'Yeah, that too. I dunno, there's no need here. I don't understand it. I'm not knocking it, though.' She paused. 'Will it all start up again when we leave?'

'I can't say, Rach. It's up to you.'

'What do you mean?'

Jack squatted down in front of her and took her hands. 'It's been good here, hasn't it?'

She nodded and he went on. 'And you haven't needed stuff and you haven't needed to cut?'

She nodded again. Jack took a deep breath. 'Promise me, when we leave here, you'll try to do without the drugs, without the cutting?'

When she looked at him this time, it was full in the face, not one of her furtive glances that slid away from his eyes.

'Will you help me? Will you stay with me and help me?'

There was a long silence, then Jack spoke again, choosing his words carefully.

'I'll help you as much as I can.'

'You swear?'

'I swear.'

She smiled then and drew her hands gently away from his. 'I got something to show you, Jack.'

He waited, curious, while she went over to the corner where they'd dumped their things and scrabbled in the backpack Yelena had given her. She took out a scrap of paper, folded over and over, the creases worn and dirty. Carefully, she unfolded it and smoothed it out.

'I've never shown this to anyone else.'

Jack frowned. 'What is it?'

'It's a letter.' She held it out to him. 'Here, have a look. Read what it says.'

Jack took it. It was written on lined paper that looked as if it had been torn out of a spiral-bound notepad. The writing was childish, in big looping script, and the spelling was so bad he had trouble deciphering what it said. As he struggled through it, the raw emotion conveyed itself to him and he felt himself tearing up.

'Who's it from?' he said at last.

'It's from Tracey,' she said. 'I could always make out her name so I knew it was from her.'

'Who's Tracey?'

'She was my friend at the home. We were friends when we were little, then she got sent away to some foster home miles away.'

'When did you get it?'

She shrugged. 'Years ago.'

'Do you know what it says?'

She shook her head. 'It was mine. I didn't want anyone else to read it.'

'Oh, Rach!'

She fiddled with her hair again. 'Will you read it to me?'

'We'll read it together. You'll be able to. Come on, look at the letters.'

Slowly she mouthed out the letters, stopping to ask if she was right.

'You're doing great. Keep going.'

He was watching her face as slowly the meaning of the words, the tone of the letter, its warmth, got through to her, and he saw the tears in her eyes.

She turned to him. 'I never had another letter, nor a phone call or nothing. I thought she'd forgotten me.'

'Perhaps she thought you'd forgotten her if you never replied.' He went on, 'It must have cost her a lot to say all that, put it all in a letter.'

Rachel nodded. 'She was a good friend. We were blood sisters when we were little.'

'You should get in touch with her.'

She sniffed. 'Nah. It's too late now.'

Jack looked at the scruffy piece of paper again. 'There's a phone number here, and she says where she's living.'

No reaction.

'It's not far from London. If you end up in London, you could get together with her.'

'Nah. She'll have moved.'

'You don't want to lose friends like that.'

She turned to him. 'That Raffi and Yelena, they were our friends too.'

He nodded. 'They gave us their numbers. You could keep in touch with them as well.'

'I haven't got a bleeding phone, have I?'

He grinned. 'You'll get another one.'

'Huh. Not as fancy as the one you chucked away.'

They didn't discuss it, but they knew when the time had come to leave. They were both cleaner than when they'd arrived at the hut, they'd been able to wash themselves and their clothes in a stream, and they were stronger and healthier.

They tidied the hut and placed the rubbish outside the door.

'Will anyone come for it?' asked Rachel.

Jack smiled at her concern.

As if it matters!

'I expect so.'

She wouldn't have cared before. Before we'd had the time in the hut.

Jack closed the door carefully behind him and they started down the track to the road, Jasper bounding beside him.

'It's been a good time, hasn't it?' Rachel said, as she ran ahead of him.

Jack nodded, then, just before he rounded a bend, he looked back, half hoping to see the hut still there, solid and real. The trees that had surrounded it were real enough, but the level ground inside the trees was bare. The hut had been there once, but not in their time. Jack squinted back at it; maybe the trees were hiding it. But he knew that wasn't true. It was the illusion he'd known it was. He glanced at his watch and saw the time and the date.

A matter of minutes since they'd arrived. How could he explain that to her?

But even so, time was running out.

They walked along the road at a brisk pace. Rachel's feet were no longer sore and Jack's chest was better. Before long they came to a crossroads with a sign.

Rachel stood and stared at it, mouthing out the letters carefully.

'B-A-M-F-O-R-D.' She sounded it out uncertainly. 'Is that right?'

'Yep. See? You'll never get lost now!'

She punched him on the arm but he could tell she was pleased.

'Hey,' she said. 'Look. There's a train.'

Jack's head jerked up. 'You're right,' he said, as he saw a train with a few carriages running along the track in the distance. 'If we keep that in sight we'll get to a railway station.'

'And then we'll get on a train to London?'

'Maybe. It's a long way and the tickets will be really expensive. He patted the pocket in his jacket. We'll need money in London.'

Unconsciously, he'd said *we*. But it wouldn't be by then, would it?

'And we've got the bleeding dog too.'

Jack put his hand on the dog's head. 'Jasper found you in the woods, Rach. We're not leaving him behind.'

If I can just get her to London . . .

They'd brought water and some food with them and they walked on, always keeping the railway line in their sight. They stopped a few times to rest.

'We're lucky,' said Rachel.

'How?'

'It's not rained once since we've been together.'

She was right. The sky remained blue, the sun shone down on them. And yet . . . and yet the grass was green; there *must* have been rain.

Jack heaved himself to his feet. 'Come on, Rach.'

'What's the hurry?'

How could he tell her that he had so little time left, that their time in the hut hadn't been real?

'You want to get to London, don't you?'

'Yeah,' she said uncertainly.

He had to prepare her.

'I may not be able to stay with you much longer,' he said.

She whipped round. 'Why? We're mates, ain't we?'

He smiled. 'I can't explain.'

She didn't say any more but he watched her scratch her arms and raise her nails to her mouth.

'Stop biting your nails,' he said.

'Don't you tell me what to do!'

At last they reached Bamford and found their way to the railway station. Jack enquired about fares to London and came back, shaking his head.

'One change, three hours, and it costs a fortune.'

'More than we've got?'

'No, but then there'd be nothing much left. You'll need some when you get to London.' He dug in his backpack. 'Look, Rach. You take the money now. You'll need it.'

She frowned. 'Why? You gonna leave me?'

I won't be able to help it.

He stuffed the money deep into her bag without answering. 'In case we get separated,' he said lamely.

Why can't I just wave a wand and get us there, find her somewhere safe?

'Shall we hide in the train toilet, then?' said Rachel.

'Mmm,' said Jack. 'Not easy with Jasper.'

Rachel bent down and stroked the dog's ears. 'I don't want to leave him,' she said.

Jack looked at her. 'Really?'

'Yeah. Well, I've got used to him.'

A bus drew up outside the station and a whole group of children disembarked.

'Look, Rach,' said Jack quickly. 'You tag onto the end of that lot, then as soon as the train comes in, find a seat near the toilet.'

'OK.' She looked uncertain. 'What about you?'

'I can look after myself. I'll get on the train, promise.'

'With Jasper?'

He nodded. 'But don't come looking for us. Just dive into the toilet if a ticket inspector comes.'

'I'm scared, Jack – I've never done nothing like this before. Where do we change trains?'

'Crewe. The train stops there; it doesn't go any further. Get off at Crewe and I'll find you there. Go on, Rach. You can do this.'

The children were all milling about inside the waiting area now and the adults with them were ushering them through onto the platform.

'I can't,' she said. 'I don't look like them.'

'Go on, quick. No one will notice. Trust me.'

He gave her a gentle push and she staggered forward. 'Sorry,' she muttered, as she dived into the milling crowd. She cast a desperate glance back at Jack and then she was carried along with the crowd.

Jack watched her go, then he followed with Jasper. Immediately a woman in railway uniform came up to him.

'You have to have a proper lead to take a dog on

the train, son,' she said, looking at the piece of string looped round Jasper's neck.

'I'm not travelling. Just seeing my sister off.'

She looked at him for longer than was comfortable, but then shrugged her shoulders and walked away.

He could see Rachel hanging around close to the other kids. She looked awkward; she was right, she didn't fit in with them.

Hope the train's on time. Someone will notice her soon.

Jack and Jasper walked to the far end of the platform where there was a covered waiting area.

Good. No one else inside.

He flattened himself against the wall and waited.

The minutes ticked by.

Hang in there, Rachel.

Then, at last, there was a general surge on the platform as the train pulled in. Jack peered round the door of the waiting area and saw that Rachel was safely on board. All the action was at her end. Parents fussing, the guard looking at his watch.

Jack made a sprint for it, through a closing door, and fell inside with Jasper. A middle-aged couple were the only people at this end of the train, and they looked up, startled, when he crashed in. He smiled at them.

It was the last carriage, so he'd have a view of any inspector coming down the train. He settled himself and persuaded Jasper to lie under his feet. The dog seemed to understand what was expected of him and he flattened himself under Jack's legs. Jack shrugged his backpack off his shoulders and sat down.

He bent to stroke Jasper's head.

If he got up to hide, he wouldn't be able to take Jasper with him.

He took his sketchpad from his backpack and started to draw, to pass the time and to stop himself worrying. He looked up and down the carriage but there was nothing that interested him, so he turned his attention to the middle-aged couple sitting across the way from him. They were bending in towards each other, talking easily together.

He envied them their closeness.

He'd been sketching for quite a time before they noticed what he was doing.

'Sorry,' he mumbled, 'I should've asked you.'

The man got up and came over to him. Instinctively Jack drew back and clasped his sketchpad to him.

'D'you mind if I see?' asked the man.

Reluctantly, Jack handed him the pad and the man studied it carefully.

'Are you an art student?'

Jack nodded. Same old lie.

'Look,' said the man, handing it to his wife. 'It's good, isn't it?'

He had drawn them as he'd seen them, their

faces animated, talking, gesticulating. It was full of movement – and of affection.

The woman took it and stared at it for a long time. Jack swallowed nervously. He didn't really want to get into a conversation; he wanted to be anonymous. He didn't want to be remembered.

She turned to her husband. 'I really like this,' she said. And then, addressing Jack, 'Would you sell it to us?'

Jack blushed. 'No. Have it. Please.'

Why did I say that?

But she was already reaching for her purse.

'No. I wouldn't hear of it,' she said firmly. 'It's very good; you mustn't just give it to us.' She opened her purse and drew out a twenty-pound note, then she stood up, came over to him and thrust it into his hand.

'I think you'll be famous one day, young man,' said her husband. 'And we shall have one of your early works!'

Jack smiled. If only they knew. He'd already had his day of fame.

'I can't take that much,' he began.

But the woman smiled. 'Of course you can. It will give us a lot of pleasure. We'll have it framed for our house.'

Jack swallowed. 'OK. If you're sure.'

'Quite sure. Now, would you sign it for me so

we know who you are and who to look out for in the future!'

The future.

Jack hesitated, then he took the sketchpad back, signed with his real name and carefully peeled off the page and handed it back to them.

I wonder if they'll ever find out? Make the connection? But then there's no reason they would.

But it pleased him to think of them enjoying his work after he'd left.

They started talking to him then, questioning him. Not in a nosey way but still, it made him nervous. He had to make up a reason for being on a train with a dog and he got himself in knots trying to explain. It sounded unconvincing.

As he was talking, he glanced at the local newspaper they'd been reading. It lay folded up on the seat opposite them.

Oh God! No!

She was there! Or rather her photo was. In the middle of the front page, Rachel's face was staring out at him!

He didn't need to read the type below the picture. He knew what it would say. His heart started to pound against his chest. He must find her!

'Sorry,' he said suddenly. 'I really need the toilet.'

He looked at Jasper, stretched out beneath the seat,

twitching in his sleep, chasing imaginary rabbits.

'Could you keep an eye on him?' He pointed at Jasper.

'Yes, of course,' said the woman. 'We'll make sure he doesn't come looking for you.'

Jack tried not to run as he went down the aisle and through into the next compartment.

Don't draw attention to yourself.

Then through the next connecting door, and the next until he saw the group of children. He scanned them to see if he could find Rachel, but there was no sign of her.

He rattled the door to one of the toilets and a voice came back. 'Hang on.'

Not Rachel.

He moved down the train, trying all the toilet doors. Either they were empty or they were occupied by someone other than Rachel. He began to panic. Where was she? He had to warn her.

Had someone already spotted her, made the connection? Were the railway people questioning her? It was a stopping train and already they had taken on more passengers and let others off.

Calm down, he told himself. *You're no good to her if you panic.*

He was at the far end of the train now, at the last toilet. He glanced back and saw a ticket inspector making his way down the aisle.

Oh God. He was trapped.

The toilet was occupied. He rattled the door.

'Rachel?' he said quietly.

No answer. He said it a bit louder and then he heard noises coming from inside and the lock slid back. The door opened a crack.

'Jack!'

'Rachel! Quick, let me in,' he whispered.

He squeezed in and shut the door behind him.

'Rach. You're in the papers . . .'

Her eyes were wide. He'd never seen her look so scared. She nodded. 'I know. I saw the picture.'

'Where? Were those kids . . . ? Did they . . .?'

She shook her head. 'I don't think so. But the woman in charge of them, she was reading the paper and I saw her look at me. What if she recognised me? Jack, it was on the front page!'

'I didn't read what it said – did you?'

Stupid question. She wouldn't have been able to read it.

'It said, *Missing.*'

He smiled at her. 'You read *missing* OK?'

She nodded.

'But who would have told the people at the paper?'

She sat down on the loo seat. 'I dunno. The home. The social worker. Adam?'

'Adam wouldn't report you missing,' said Jack.

'No?'

'No. He'd be in all sorts of trouble if he did that, wouldn't he?'

'I s'pose.'

Jack looked down at her. 'It won't be long before we're in London.'

She nodded. 'I can't go back now.' She paused. 'Will they find me in London, Jack? Now I'm in the papers and that?'

Jack squatted down on the floor in front of her and took her hand in his.

'If we can get to London, I know where you can go to be safe. Once you're there, it will be OK, I promise.'

He fingered the banknote in his pocket. Enough to get them across London by Tube. He wouldn't tell her about the money he'd been given. Not yet.

Suddenly there was a thump on the door.

They both froze, staring at each other, helpless.

'Anyone in there? I need to see your ticket.'

'Say something,' mouthed Jack.

'Yeah.' Rachel's voice was faint.

A voice from outside. 'You OK, love?'

'I just got stomach cramps. It's my period.'

'Ah.' There was an embarrassed silence.

'It's OK.' She paused. 'I'm with the holiday club from Bamford.'

'OK.'

There was the sound of feet shuffling outside the door and then walking away.

'Brilliant!' said Jack, letting out his breath. 'You should get an Oscar for that!'

She smiled weakly and he could see the strain in her face.

'It's not long till we get to Crewe,' he said. 'We can catch the fast train to London from there.'

She didn't answer. He started to take off his hoodie, banging his elbows against the side of the toilet walls.

'What are you doing?'

'Wear this,' he said, handing it to her. 'It'll hide your face, at least.'

Gingerly, she took it from him. 'Yuk, I'm not wearing this manky . . .' she began.

He made a despairing face at her. 'This is no time to go all fashion conscious on me, Rach!'

'Yeah. OK.'

'Look. I'd better go back to Jasper.'

'Oh yeah! I'd forgotten him. Is he OK?'

Jack nodded. 'For now.'

'What shall I do, Jack? Stay in here?'

'I don't know. You can't stay in here all the time or someone'll come and see if you're OK. Go and sit down and pretend to be reading or something.'

'You got a book?'

Jack dug in his backpack, found a paperback and shoved it into her hands.

'What's it about – in case anyone asks?'

Jack grinned. 'A boy, a girl and a dog,' he said.

'Eh?'

Jack unbolted the door and glanced outside. There was no one waiting and no sign of the inspector.

'See you at Crewe,' he whispered. 'It's not far.'

'How will I know it's Crewe?'

'This train stops there, doesn't go any further. And they'll announce it, too'

'OK.'

He shut the door quietly on her as she sat, white-faced, clutching his book in one hand and chewing the nails on the other.

He made his way back to his seat and, as he approached, Jasper's nose came out from underneath and he could hear the tail thumping on the floor of the carriage. He smiled at the couple.

'Thank you,' said Jack gratefully.

Ten minutes later, the train started slowing down. The middle-aged couple gathered their belongings and stood up. The woman put her hand on Jack's arm.

'Thank you for the drawing,' she said.

'It's OK,' mumbled Jack.

Jack waited until most people were off the train and there were crowds on the platform, then he and

Jasper jumped out of the carriage.

He didn't think anyone had noticed them – not anyone official, anyway – though he did see one of the holiday club kids turning round to stare and point at the dog.

He looked away, scanning the crowd for Rachel; Rachel wearing his hoodie. He felt naked without it.

Jack

before

'Posh boy!'

I'd known it would happen. As soon as I stepped into the classroom at the new school and looked around, I knew they'd come after me.

I tried to change my accent, tried to keep my head down.

It didn't work. I was marked from the start. I didn't fit in.

The bullying was low key at first. Mimicking the way I spoke, bumping into me in the corridors, hiding my books. Laughing at me, whispering, pointing.

Then the notes – and the threats.

'Think you're better than us, you posh boff?'

'We know where you live, you loser.'

The gang was the worst. Egging each other on, making each other brave, showing off, bragging. Seeing who could throw the worst insults at me. The other kids were scared of the gang, too scared to stand up to them by befriending me so they left me alone and smiled weakly at the taunts flung at me, silently colluding, embarrassed, walking away from me, leaving me on my own.

I'd tried not to react. Mostly I could blank out the insults but sometimes they said something that hit home and I'd flinch. They could see when they'd found a raw spot.

The physical stuff started when they tired of my silence, of my refusal to react. It usually happened in the toilets, out of sight of the teachers.

They never hit me where it showed; never on my face. But there were plenty of other targets.

Day after day I had to psyche myself up to walk through those gates knowing what lay ahead.

I couldn't tell anyone. I hid it all – from the teachers, from Mum. Most of all from Mum. She had enough to worry about.

Chapter 10

He couldn't wait on the platform any longer. The crowd was beginning to thin out and someone might question him. Quickly, Jack led Jasper away, out onto the concourse, then he stopped and leaned against a pillar.

Where was she? Surely she could see him? He and Jasper couldn't be difficult to spot.

He waited with increasing anxiety. What had happened to her? She must have realised that this was Crewe. He'd told her the train ended here. He looked up at the big overhead display showing times of trains, and noticed that there was a fast train to London in about ten minutes. The less time spent hanging around here, the better – less time for someone to recognise Rachel, though they'd have to get onto a train without tickets again. It wouldn't be easy.

Jack's stomach rumbled. Dragging Jasper behind

him, he went over to a food booth and spent some of his drawing money on a couple of sandwiches and some bottled drink and then continued looking for Rachel.

The time ticked by. He'd given up the idea of the fast train when suddenly Rachel was at his side.

'Where the hell were you? I've been looking all over.'

'Rachel! Couldn't you see me? Not many people around with a dog like Jasper are there?' He felt cross and tired.

'I'm telling you, I couldn't see you.'

She was trembling and he realised, again, how scared she was. She'd been crying and she rubbed her eyes with the back of her fist.

She really couldn't see me. Is it happening already? Surely it couldn't happen now?

'I saw the dog,' she sniffed.

'What?'

'I saw Jasper. At least I think it was him.' She paused. 'I thought you'd left him. Thought you'd left both of us and buggered off.'

'Rach, for God's sake. You know I wouldn't do that.' Jack glanced up at the overhead display again.

Damn. They'd missed the fast train now.

'Where were you?' Rachel persisted.

I don't know, do I?

Aloud he said, 'I bought us some food. He handed

her one of the sandwiches and began to eat the other himself.

She snatched it from him. 'What did you use for money? Thought you'd given me all our money. Did you nick some?'

He told her about the couple on the train. He knew she'd go on questioning him if he didn't.

She sniffed and started to talk with her mouth full.

'What?' said Jack.

She swallowed and then grabbed one of the bottles of drink from him.

'You should do more of that. Drawing and getting money for it.'

'Hmm,' said Jack.

Bit late for that.

Rachel pushed the hood away from her face.

'Don't do that, Rach,' whispered Jack, pushing it back over her head. 'Someone might recognise you.'

'Yeah, I'm a celebrity! Whoa!'

He was amazed at how quickly her mood had changed. It was hard to keep up with her sometimes. Down in the depths one minute and then manic and living for the moment the next. He watched her wolf down the food.

'Rach.'

He had to tell her. Make her realise.

'Yeah?'

What's the use? She won't understand. How could she?

'Try to keep close by me,' he said lamely. 'Don't lose sight of me.'

Don't lose sight of me. But it will happen – is happening. Please let me get her to safety first. Don't let me fail.

She looked at him and frowned. 'Sure.' Then she wiped her mouth with the back of the sleeve of his hoodie. 'But we separate once we're on the train, right? Like we did before?'

'Yeah. We'll see. We've got to get on the train first.'

'Yeah, how are we gonna do that?'

He'd been wondering that himself. It was harder here. There were ticket barriers to go through before you got onto the platforms. He looked around, sizing up the place. There was a big covered walkway that spanned the railway lines, taking passengers from one side to the other. Maybe there was some way . . .

Jack looked up at the display board again. Rachel followed his gaze.

'Hey,' she said suddenly. 'That says *London*.' She pointed to a word that had just flashed up.

Jack nodded. 'Yep. London Euston,' he said. 'Well done, Rach. You're doing brilliantly. What platform number?'

'Three,' she said, punching his arm. 'I know the numbers! I've always known my numbers.'

He smiled. 'OK, that's the next London train. Goes

from platform three in fifteen minutes.'

But it was a slow train. Too many stops, too long. Too much time for someone to recognise her and they couldn't rely on finding another group of kids she could hide amongst. It might be better to wait for the next fast train.

The crowds were thinning out. A lot of people had dispersed.

Jack chewed the last of his sandwich and stood up.

'Come on, Rach. We'll have a snoop round. See if we can find a way to get onto the platform without paying.'

Rachel looked down at Jasper and fed him the last of her sandwich. 'It's all your fault,' she said, stroking his nose. 'You stand out a bloody mile.'

They were walking off when Rachel stopped. A policeman was coming towards them, talking into the radio clipped onto his uniform. He was looking straight at Rachel as he spoke. Rachel froze and clutched Jack's hand, instinctively turning away from the man's gaze.

There was nowhere to run; the policeman was suddenly right beside them.

He looked them up and down. 'You kids OK?' he asked.

Jack spoke up quickly. 'Yeah, we're just waiting for a train to come in. It's our mum, she's coming up from London.'

How quickly the lies come.

'Which train's she on, then?'

Jack's eyes swivelled to the display board. 'The one coming in ten minutes,' he said quickly.

The policeman had noticed his darting eyes, his desperate glance up to the board.

Damn! He knows I'm lying. Go away!

But the man continued to stand there, solid, unconvinced.

'This your sister?'

'Yeah.'

'What's her name, then?'

Jack scowled. It wasn't any of his business, was it? Better not be rude.

'Tracey,' he said quickly. And he felt Rachel squeeze his hand.

'Tracey,' said the policeman slowly. 'And what's your name son?'

'Jack.'

No one knows me as Jack.

'And you say you're meeting your mum.'

Jack could feel himself blushing. Damn. He nodded.

'She been away, has she – down south?'

Jack nodded again.

There was a heavy silence.

'This your dog?'

Jack could feel Rachel was beginning to tremble

beside him. He had to get her away.

'Yes,' he said.

The policeman bent down and stroked Jasper's head. 'You should get him a proper collar and lead.'

'He stays by me,' muttered Jack. 'He doesn't stray.'

The policeman straightened up. 'Even so. What if he got lost?'

Jack began to sweat. Would this questioning never stop? He looked up at the display board again. The train from London was due in in a few minutes.

'We'd better go,' he said. 'Mum's train . . .'

'I'll come with you, make sure you get there safely.'

Rachel couldn't keep quiet any longer. Her head jerked up and the hood fell back, exposing her face.

'We're OK,' she said. 'Leave us alone.'

Oh, Rach!

Quickly she pulled the hood up again but not before the policeman had taken a good look at her.

At that moment, the policeman's radio kicked into life and he bent his head to listen and respond.

Jack jerked on Jasper's piece of string, turned and ran, pulling Rachel with him. When he looked back, he saw the policeman running after them, speaking into his radio.

Oh God, he's getting reinforcements. He knows who Rachel is!

Jack had no firm plan. Perhaps they should have

stayed, brazened it out. But then the policeman had seen her face. The face that was suddenly so recognisable.

They ran blindly, dodging trollies and passengers pulling suitcases behind them, off the main concourse, up steps and over the covered walkway towards the other side of the railway tracks. There was no one else using the walkway and their footsteps echoed in the space. Jack's chest was beginning to hurt again and he knew he couldn't keep this up. 'We've got to hide somewhere,' he panted.

Then Rachel stopped suddenly, jerking on his hand. 'Look,' she whispered.

He saw where she was pointing. There were some big, freestanding advertising hoardings along the side of the walkway, secured to the wall by metal struts.

'We could get behind them,' she said.

They could hear shouting. There was no time for indecision. They both squeezed behind the hoardings. Jasper didn't even struggle when Jack picked him up.

'Climb higher, so your feet don't show,' said Rachel.

They flattened themselves behind the hoardings, legs splayed, leaning back against the wall behind. All three of them were badly squashed.

Jack tried to stroke Jasper's head but he couldn't reach it.

Please don't make a noise, boy.

They heard the sound of footsteps pounding up the

stairs now. They could see nothing but it was obvious that there were several people in pursuit of them. People shouting, directing.

'They came this way. I saw them.' Was that the voice of the policeman who'd spoken to them?

'Yeah, they must be over the other side by now. Come on. They won't get far. Not with that dog.'

The footsteps didn't slow up as they passed the hoardings but continued on, and they heard them fading away down the steps the other side.

Rachel managed to peer round the edge.

'There's no one here,' she whispered.

Jack squeezed out, still holding Jasper. 'OK. Let's double back and try to get on a train. Any train. One that's leaving the station.'

'You sure?'

'No. Just can't think of anything else to do.'

They ran back the way they had come.

'Down there. Look!' said Jack.

There was a crackling announcement coming over the loudspeakers. 'The train now standing at platform one is departing for London Euston, calling at . . .'

'We'll try it,' said Jack.

There were other people running for the train but they all had tickets that they were feeding into the barrier gates.

'Duck under the barrier, Rach. I'll distract the guard.'

'Will you –?'

'Yes, I'll come. Somehow I'll come. Wait for me at Euston. I'll be there, I promise.'

He tied the dog to a railing out of sight and ran up to the guard. 'I've lost my ticket,' he began. 'I can't find it anywhere.'

The guard took in his shabby T-shirt and scuffed trainers.

'You got money for another ticket, son?'

Jack nodded. Out of the corner of his eye he saw Rachel safely on the other side running for the nearest carriage and leaping in just as the doors were shutting. He breathed freely again.

The guard was saying something. Jack wasn't concentrating. The train was beginning to draw out of the station.

'This one's leaving, son, but there's another one for London soon.' He pointed to the ticket office on the other side of the station. 'Go over there. They'll sort you out.' He patted Jack's back. 'And if you find your ticket later, you can get a refund,' he said kindly. 'And –' He stopped abruptly, frowning. 'Where did he go?' he muttered, staring at the place where Jack had been.

Once he'd seen that Rachel was safely on the train, Jack walked away. It would be easier now. At least for him. No one would notice him, and only the dog would know he was there.

He slipped easily through the crowds and collected Jasper. He took the string off him and let it slip to the ground. 'We've got to be really careful, boy,' he whispered. 'We've got to hide you somewhere till I can sneak you onto a train. They'll be looking out for you.'

Jasper slunk away and hid under a seat. Jack crouched down. 'Stay, boy. Stay there till I come back.'

He fondled Jasper's ears and then left. Such a quiet creature. A silent hunter who knew when to make himself invisible. Jack knew he was there, tucked under the seat, right at the back, but even he couldn't see him now.

And now no one could see Jack. He'd forgotten how it felt to move unseen in a crowd.

It would be so easy if it was just him. He could slip onto any train he chose. But with a living, breathing, all-too-substantial dog, it was a different matter.

The next train from London was due in twenty minutes. Jack studied the electronic board carefully. Then a train left for London ten minutes later from the same platform. Must be the same train. He'd have to get Jasper on board and find a place to hide him. But how?

He wandered over to the platform where the London train was due to come in, slipped unseen through the barriers again and walked up and down the platform. It was too risky. Someone was sure to spot an unaccompanied dog walking up the platform and getting onto the train. He sat down and dangled his legs over the edge of the platform looking down at the rails beneath.

I'm supposed to look out for Rachel. I should have left Jasper and gone with her. Someone would have looked after him.

But he couldn't leave him. Jasper had been abandoned once already and he wasn't going to leave him again. He knew where Jasper should be, where he could be sure he would be safe, but it would mean taking him to London too.

He stared down at the rails again, looking at the huge buffers at the platform end. The incoming train would come right up to them, wouldn't it? He stood up and peered round the corner, where the platform ended. If he could get the dog to jump down there and creep under the train once it was in the station, if he could do this unnoticed when the passengers were disembarking, then maybe . . .

He walked back to the bench where Jasper was hiding. People were sitting on it now. Good. Jasper was well hidden. Jack went round to the back of the bench and lay down on the ground. 'Jasper!' He could just make out Jasper's shape through the iron legs of the bench and saw his tail wag. Jack wriggled closer and stretched out a hand to stroke the wiry blond hair on the dog's back.

'Just a few more minutes, boy,' he said. But only Jasper could hear him.

The train was due. People on the bench started to shuffle, collect their belongings, stand up.

Jack heard the announcement. 'The train now arriving at platform one . . .'

People were surging towards the platform now.

He whistled to Jasper. 'Come on, boy. Follow me. Quick.'

Jasper wriggled out from under the bench and followed Jack as he ducked and weaved between passengers and luggage, going round a pillar to where the train had come to a stop. Then he pointed to the rails and Jasper immediately jumped down, looking up questioningly as soon as he landed.

Will he understand? Will he know what I want him to do?

Jack watched as the dog stood, uncertain, still looking up at him. Jack started to move along the platform, gesturing for Jasper to follow. There were a few heart-stopping moments when Jasper was in full sight, if anyone had chosen to look down onto the rails. But he suddenly moved off, slinking unseen beneath the body of the train. Jack walked along the edge, keeping him in his sight, until he reached the far end of the train. Then he called softly to the dog and Jasper stopped and stared up from beneath a carriage, his eyes bright in the gloom.

Jack waited until the last passenger had left the carriage.

'Now, boy! Quick!'

Jasper leaped up onto the platform and Jack pointed to an open door. With one bound, Jasper was inside the carriage, immediately finding himself a position tucked well under a seat.

Jack breathed again. He got in after him and sat down.

'I can't give you anything now, Jasper,' he whispered, wondering again why an animal could sense his presence while a human couldn't. 'Later, when we get to Euston and find Rachel, we'll get you some food.'

But for now, he was as insubstantial as the draught of wind that sent an empty styrofoam cup rolling over and over down the platform, until it fell over the edge and onto the rails.

Rachel

before

It was easy enough to bunk off from the home. A group of us would go into town and hang out. But I was too wild then, even for them, always pushing the limits, drinking more than anyone else, ending up legless in the gutter, puking my guts out. Then there was the night when they left me. The police had been trying to round us up and the rest of them had run away. I was kicking off, lashing out at some copper, off my head, when this guy had come up. I'd seen him hanging around a few times. He'd smiled at me and I guess I thought he fancied me. He was good looking. Dark. With these big brown eyes and thick hair. Just as the police were picking me up, he comes up and says, 'I'll get her home, officer. I know where she lives.'

Well, I was so out of my skull I couldn't think straight. All I knew was I didn't want to end up in some police cell for the night so when they asked me if I knew him I must have muttered something cos they went away. Probably dead relieved not to have to cope with another drunken teenager.

He was great at first. Really loving and that. I couldn't believe it. Thought I'd died and gone to heaven. No one had ever been that nice to me. I didn't like his friends so much but what the hell, I just had to put up with them. I couldn't give a toss what they thought. Then he said I could move into his flat. It was a bit of a dosshouse and there were people coming and going all the time, but he was there with me and that's all I cared about.

I thought he loved me. I thought he'd always look out for me. But he fed me so much stuff I was high most of the time, out of it.

Chapter 11

Rachel hid in the toilet, biting her nails down even further, wrapping Jack's hoodie round her.

I'm never going to see him again. He's left me this time. What am I going to do when I get to London?

Over and over again she opened her purse and looked at the money in it. Jack had given her all their money. She was still hungry and once, when she'd peered out of the toilet, she'd seen a guy going up and down the aisle pushing a trolley with food on it, but she was too scared to try to buy anything from it.

Would they be looking for her when she got to London? She was sure that the woman on the train at Bamford had recognised her from the picture in the paper. Would she tell the police and would they phone ahead, tell the coppers up the line to look out for her?

Christ, Jack. Where are you? What am I going to do?

She sat on the toilet seat, curled up, hugging her

knees, as the train sped on its way south. She kept telling herself she must stay awake, keep alert to anyone banging on the door, but fatigue overwhelmed her and she dropped off only to be jerked awake suddenly.

'You OK in there?'

A woman's voice. A ticket inspector? Some impatient passenger?

Rachel groaned in response. 'Being sick . . .' That should send the nosey woman away, whoever she was.

There was a pause. 'I'll go and find someone to help.'

Oh God, that's just what I need. Some bleeding do-gooder.

She heard her walk away. Rachel uncurled herself and quietly unlocked the door, looking up and down the corridor. She could see a woman walking down the aisle.

Bet that's her.

Silently, Rachel slunk out of the toilet and walked in the opposite direction.

She found a corner seat in the next carriage, which was right at the back of the train, and turned her face to the window, the hood pulled down.

How much longer? When does this frigging train get to London? What am I going to do when I get there – if someone doesn't suss me out before then?

The voices in her head had been whispering for most of the journey but now they began to get louder and louder. She put her hands on either side of her face and rocked to and fro. But this time it didn't work. They were clamouring to be heard, shouting in her brain.

And the tune again, breaking through the voices. She hummed along to it, trying to drown them out, trying to think them away.

He said I was good at singing. Jack said I had a good voice.

She hung on to that, a fragile spider's thread, a shred of self esteem. But the flare of hope died almost immediately.

Who am I kidding? Anyone can hold a tune.

She slumped back in her seat and continued to stare out of the window, scowling, the voices in her head coming back with full force, drowning out the tune. She banged her head against the window. God, would they never go away! Conflicting commands, some telling her to do stupid things, trash the seats, bang her head until it bled.

Bleeding.

She felt inside her bag for the razor. She'd not done it for a while. She'd promised Jack, but she couldn't stand the tension; this was the only way. Her hands were shaking as she drew out the razor. Such a little thing, so easy to hide. And such a shiny, sharp blade. Her sweaty hands were shaking so much that it took her several goes to grip the blade properly. She rolled up her sleeve and closed her eyes as she cut deep and felt the tension seep out of her. Normally she would have had a load of tissues to mop up the blood, but this time she didn't bother. She opened her eyes again and held her arm out, watching the blood dribble down her arm and onto the fabric of the seat.

The voices were much quieter now, dying down to whispers, and the tune softer. Then a new voice, a different one was coming through. She frowned.

Quiet, insistent, calm. But she couldn't make out the words. She closed her eyes again and tried to concentrate.

Hang in there, Rach. Don't give up.

She sat bolt upright and looked around. No, not real, then. He was in her head. He was speaking to her in her head!

For a few moments she sat there, trembling, the flow of blood down her arm slowing to a trickle. Then the voice spoke again.

Wait for me.

It *was* Jack!

Bloody hell, he can get in my head now!

But this wasn't a scary voice. She leaned back, calming down gradually, and thought back to their time at the hut in the woods, the time when she'd begun to suspect.

She didn't bother to wipe the blood from her arm but rolled down her sleeve to cover it and took some deep breaths.

She'd known then, in the woods, but she'd blocked it out. Told herself it was some sort of dream, something like the highs she'd had when she'd been on the hard drugs. When nothing was real. But she knew.

She'd never dared question him after that. If he was who she thought he was – she couldn't go there.

She blinked and shifted in her seat, and as she did so she saw the woman coming back down the aisle with some sort of official in tow.

Shit. They're going to find me.

She couldn't go anywhere. There was nowhere to go. She was right at the end of the last carriage. If she tried to run for it, she'd have to barge past them.

The voices in her head started up again.

Run, run, run away. Jump.

She looked this way and that, up at the window.

Jump!

Why not? She could do it. That would solve everything wouldn't it? No more hassle. End it all. But as soon as she put her hand up to open the window, she realised she wouldn't be able to squeeze out anyway. It only opened at the top, just a little way. She dropped her hand into her lap.

Keep calm, the voice ordered.

The woman and the inspector, or whoever it was, were closer now.

'In this toilet, here.' The woman's voice was strident, bossy. 'I think someone's very unwell.'

Rachel recognised that kind of voice. The voice of someone used to being in charge, making decisions for others. Time and again she'd heard the same confident tone – from social workers, ologists, carers, teachers. Instinctively, she withdrew a little further into Jack's hoodie, curled up even tighter.

They had stopped at the toilet.

'Oh.' The woman's loud voice as she opened the toilet door. 'Oh, it's empty.'

Then the man mumbling something.

They'll see me. They'll walk further on, looking for me.

Every muscle was tense as Rachel waited. She didn't listen, just heard the rhythm of their conversation. Then, at last, the footsteps went back the way they had come. She let out a long breath.

How much longer?

She looked up at the sign above her head. It flashed up the names of stations – the words were going by very quickly, but she focused on them, thinking of Jack's patient teaching. And as she stared at the constantly moving letters, she realised that the same words were repeating over and over. Before, there'd been masses of words, names of the stations, she supposed. She'd lost count of the times the train had stopped to let people off, take people on. Now there were only two left. She concentrated on the one that came up second. She recognised the word *London* and slowly mouthed out the word beside it. Euston! She got it at last. Euston Station. The end of the line. One more stop and then she'd be there.

And then?

Her stomach cramped. How would she get off the train? Would there be people checking tickets? This time she'd have to sneak out on her own. And what if someone recognised her?

She'd always wanted to go to London, though, hadn't she?

Yeah. But now I'm nearly there, what'll I do? What'll I do if Jack never comes?

Wait for me.

The voice in her head again.

She started to chew her nails. How did she know he'd come? He'd only got the money from his drawing – and he had that stupid dog. He'd probably already been stopped and put off the train – or arrested.

She dug her hands into the pockets of Jack's hoodie and leaned against the window.

But if he was who she thought he was, he'd manage. Somehow he'd manage. But the dog?

She sighed. The train was slowing down. If she'd

got it right, then this was the last stop before Euston. As she had at every stop, she scanned the crowds on the platform, her heart speeding up every time she saw anyone in uniform. There weren't many people getting on here and she couldn't see any police; the only official people were railway staff.

Doors slammed, a man blew a whistle and the train lurched forward again, slowly gathering momentum.

She let out her breath and unclenched her fists. Just one more stop.

It began raining as the train neared London, lashing the train windows. She peered up into the sky and saw the leaden clouds overhead. It hadn't rained for weeks. Ever since she'd been with Jack it had been warm and sunny, the earth cracked and dry when they were out in the country – or had she imagined it? Had it really been so sunny? What was real? Was this real, this nightmare journey, running away from Adam, from the police – from everything?

The train began to slow down and she tried to think. Should she get off with everyone else and try to blend in with the crowd? Or stay on the train, hiding somewhere, until . . . until what? She didn't know what happened in a big station like this. Did they check your ticket? Were there more people in uniform ready to grab her, return her to her former life, to the home, the gang, the drugs?

Is that what you want, Rach?

The voice in her head again.

She shook her head violently. She'd come this far, but what now?

Trust me.

But you're not bleeding here, are you?

Then nothing. No voices, not even the background whispers. Silence.

The train drew into the station. People stood up and grabbed their bags. Doors opened.

For a few moments, Rachel didn't move, watching as passengers pushed forward anxiously to get off the train, continue their journey, go to their homes.

Homes.

I'll never have a home.

Then, suddenly, she made up her mind. She slung her bag over her shoulder and rose to her feet. As she glanced down at her arm she saw that Jack's hoodie was stained with blood.

Sorry, Jack. I couldn't help it.

Then she was up, pushing with the others to get to the door, keeping the hood up to hide her face, being swept along with the crowd heading for the barrier. She stared ahead.

Don't notice me. Please, no one notice me.

The crowd slowed as it approached the barrier. People scrabbled for their tickets, hands in pockets, in wallets, ready to feed them into the waiting machines.

Rachel's heart started to beat faster. She should have realised there'd be barriers here too. She hung back, her eyes darting this way and that. There was no way off the platform except through those damned machines. She could duck under but there were a couple of blokes there too, both in railway uniform. She looked back up the platform; hardly anyone there now, just an elderly woman struggling with her luggage.

Help her!

His voice again.

What?

Help her.

Rachel stood, irresolute. It made no sense. If she went back someone would see her, notice her, away from the crowd.

The voice was louder now, more insistent.

Help her.

She found herself fighting her way back, against the flow of the crowd.

What am I doing?

She reached the old lady, noticed that she was limping badly, her face creased into worry lines as she tried to roll two suitcases along the platform and, at the same time, keep a huge shoulder bag from slipping down onto the ground.

She looked up, startled, when Rachel came up to her.

'Here,' said Rachel gruffly. 'Let me help.'

The woman stared at her and for a moment Rachel felt her hostility, suspicion. She was about to turn away and run back when the woman's face relaxed and she smiled.

'Thank you, love,' she said. 'If you could take the cases, that'd be a great help.'

Rachel nodded. They were heavy but at least they had wheels. She started dragging them behind her, staying close to the side of the woman.

'Ever so kind of you,' said the woman. 'It's not often young people offer to help. I really appreciate it.'

'S'all right,' muttered Rachel, her eyes on the barrier ahead. Most of the people had gone through; there were just a few stragglers left.

As they approached, one of the railway officials opened up the widest gate on the barrier to let them through.

Rachel kept her head down and stuck close behind the woman, her heart beating so loudly she could swear others could hear it.

The woman put her bag down and started scrabbling inside.

'Oh dear,' she said. 'I know I've got our tickets somewhere.'

OUR tickets? Had she meant to say that? Did she realise?
The man at the barrier smiled. 'Don't worry,

madam,' he said. 'I believe you.'

And then they were through, onto the main concourse.

OUR tickets?

Rachel shook her head and the woman turned to her. 'Thank you so much, lovey,' she repeated.

Rachel could see two policemen coming their way. To check the crowds coming off the train? To find her?

Her mouth was dry. She swallowed. 'Can I take these somewhere for you?' she managed, her eyes still on the policemen.

The woman smiled. 'Thank you, dear. If you can manage to take them to that café, I'll buy you a drink and a sandwich – if you have time.'

Rachel's stomach rumbled. She had time.

As they trailed the luggage over to the café at a snail's pace, the old lady wittered on about her son coming to meet her. They were going to meet up at the café, she said, in half an hour, when her son finished work.

Rachel wasn't listening. If she could pretend to be attached to this old lady for half an hour, perhaps the police wouldn't spot her.

Rachel guarded the luggage while the old lady limped up to the counter and placed an order. When it came, Rachel wolfed down two large slices of cake and a hot chocolate while her companion watched her, drinking slowly from a mug of tea.

'Are you being met by someone, too?'

Rachel shook her head, her mouth full of cake. When she was able to speak, she'd considered her answer. 'My boyfriend's coming on another train,' she said shortly.

The old woman gave her a long look.

What? Do I look as if I couldn't get a boyfriend? What's she thinking?

'Tell me about him,' said the lady, holding her mug between her hands. 'What's he like?'

Rachel stared at her. She thought briefly of Adam. Then she started to describe Jack.

'He's clever,' she said. 'And ever so gentle. And he's kind to me, looks out for me.'

There. She'd said it. Acknowledged it. However much they rowed, however much they irritated each other, it was true. He did look out for her, but he wouldn't be able to now, would he?

The old woman looked surprised, then she smiled and put her hand over Rachel's.

'He sounds lovely,' she said. 'You make sure you look out for him too.'

Rachel looked down at her lap. She couldn't tell this woman the truth. She couldn't tell anyone the truth. She'd probably never see Jack again.

Soon, the woman's son arrived and gathered her

up, flinging her bag over his shoulders and rolling the two suitcases easily behind him. They both thanked her again.

'Are you sure you'll be all right?' asked the woman for the hundredth time.

'Yeah. He'll be here soon. I'll be OK.'

But as soon as they had left, she knew she'd have to find somewhere to hide. Being with someone else had given her some protection but now she was alone.

While she'd been talking to the woman she'd been glancing about her, eyes darting this way and that. There was one policeman who had been standing outside the café for some time and now he was joined by another.

Rachel turned away from them and gripped her empty mug. It was only a matter of time. She had to get away.

Would Jack come? Would he be able to come?

Wait for me.

But the voice in her head was faint.

She couldn't wait there. The waitress was already eyeing her, giving off the familiar vibes of contempt. And the two policemen could come in any moment.

She glanced around. There was no back way. No other way to leave the café – just by the front, the way they'd come in. She turned to look at the policemen again; oh God, they'd been joined by another – a woman this time. She knew then. She knew what they were going to do.

Where's Jack's voice now, for God's sake? Tell me what to do!

But there was no reassuring voice in her head. Even the whispers had deserted her.

Just the tune. Faintly at first and she found her eyes drawn back to the police. Someone had come up to them, shouting, brandishing a bottle. A drunk. A noisy drunk woman.

The tune was so loud now. It was telling her, directing her.

The three police were trying to calm the woman down but she was lashing out at them, swearing.

Something about the woman made Rachel look at her and, just for a moment, their eyes connected. The tune thundered in her head. Who was she? Could she be . . . ?

Is it her? Is she *looking out for me too?*

She had no time to wonder, she had to take her chance, now, while the police were distracted. Rachel slipped out of her seat, eased round the corner of the doorway and ran as fast as she could, out of the station, onto the wet London pavements, into the rain sleeking her hair, soaking her clothes, until she found a dark doorway and slumped down, crying in fright. She fumbled in her bag and took out the sketch of the dog that Jack had given her, hoping that having something of his close to her would bring him back. It was then that she noticed the signature at the bottom. The name wasn't Jack, even she could see that. It was written clearly in bold letters. Another name – she was right! She knew for sure who he was now. She held the drawing tightly to her chest.

Jack

before

I think I went a bit mad when I saw those bruises. Something in my head exploded. The hard time I was getting at school, the horrible house in the horrible street in the middle of a city I hated. And then seeing my mum like that, scared and trapped. It all built up. It was all Kevin's fault and at that moment, I wanted to kill him. I didn't say anything when I saw the bruises all the way up her arm, just looked away, but before I could change my mind, I ran up the stairs, went straight to my room and phoned the police.

Big mistake. Of course, when the police came round, Mum denied it all. Kevin was there, a protective arm round her shoulders, squeezing her just a bit too tightly.

He knew it was me. Who else would it be? And from that moment, he planned his revenge. I was sick with fear, knowing he would choose his moment. I tried never to be alone in the house with him, but it wasn't easy. The days went by. I didn't sleep, I couldn't do my school work. He was biding his time, waiting for the right moment. It was the waiting that was doing my head in.

Up till then, he'd never really hurt me but I knew it would happen, sooner or later. There were whispered threats, out of Mum's hearing. 'You sneaky little poof, I'll sort you out. You just wait.'

Every day I had to watch my back, make sure Mum and the twins were in the house, not be alone with him. Then one evening, I slipped up. I'd forgotten that Mum was teaching an evening class and that the twins were playing at a friend's house.

When I got home the house was empty, but a little while later Kevin came in drunk.

I took a knife from the kitchen and went upstairs to my room. I lay on my bed, the knife hidden under my pillow, hoping he'd not realise I was in the house, hoping Mum might come home early. Then I heard his heavy tread on the stairs and a grunt as he flung open my bedroom door.

I still try to forget what happened that night. The stink of drink, the sound of Kevin's harsh laughter, the terror and the pain as he hit me, again and again, then twisting round, grabbing the knife from under the pillow and thrusting it up into his chest.

I couldn't believe it when he staggered back, blood pouring from him, clutching his chest and I'd watched, horrified, as he slumped onto the floor, twitching, and then, finally, lying horribly, grotesquely still.

Had I killed him? If I had, I hadn't meant to. I'd just wanted the pain to stop.

For several moments I couldn't move, then, whimpering with fear, I'd snatched up a few clothes, my phone, some cash and my sketchpad, and stuffed them in my old backpack, the one I couldn't bear to part with, the one I'd used when Dad and I had gone hill walking together. Then I crept out of the house.

Once I was a few streets away I sent a text to Mum. *I'm leaving home.*

And I disappeared.

Chapter 12

The dog was the worry. Not him. No one could see Jack now, no one could sense his presence even – except the dog. It certainly made travelling easier but it also meant that his time had run out. He'd experimented, pushed the limits with Rachel, stayed with her far too long. He should have left her at the farm, left it to Raffi and the others to protect her. But now he'd have to finish the job, be sure she was safe. Absently, he stroked Jasper, feeling the broken coat, the rough lurcher hair beneath his fingers. Could Jasper feel him? He liked to think so. The dog had hardly shifted since they'd set off, crawling under the seat, belly flat, making himself invisible. He understood what was expected of him. Deep in his gypsy genes he knew when he needed to keep quiet.

The train he'd managed to board was only forty-five minutes behind Rachel's train. But anything could happen in that time. What if the police had picked her up? What if she'd not got the messages he'd tried to send her? What if she had run off, scared?

Don't let me mess up now. Just let me get her safe.

But he knew he was losing control.

He tried to send another message to her. 'Hang in there, Rach. I'm coming. Trust me.' He didn't think it would work. He was getting too far away.

When at last the train drew into Euston Station, he was one of the first off, though no one saw him. He waited for the dog to follow, slinking so quietly out from his hiding place, following the crowd and then jumping down under the train, walking on the tracks, hidden from view. By the time he re-emerged, everyone was surging towards the barrier and no one saw him leap up and squeeze round a pillar onto the main concourse.

Jack caught him up. 'Clever lad,' he said. Jasper looked up and wagged his tail. Could he see him? Did his heightened animal senses include sight denied to humans? Or did he merely sense his presence?

Jack moved off, Jasper at his heels. People were hurrying by, places to go, people to see. Only a sharp-eyed policeman spotted the dog, trotting purposefully forward, apparently unaccompanied.

There was no sign of Rachel, but then Jack had expected her to be hiding somewhere.

He summoned up all his energy to send another message to connect with the voices in her head. He must be closer to her now; it might get through.

He darted into cafés and shops, peered into dark corners. He was no longer restricted and he moved so fast and with such lightness that Jasper could hardly keep up.

Nothing. He stood still. He didn't need to rest now, there was no pain any more, no hacking cough. Now he could go anywhere at speed, but where? Where had she gone?

Out of the station, up the steps and into the street. It was raining hard but he felt nothing – just noticed how Jasper's coat was heavy with moisture and that he shook every now and then to rid himself of it, spraying fine droplets in an arc around Jack.

He stopped for a moment, trying to think. If she'd left the station, where would she go? She didn't know London; she had no friends.

Friendless, vulnerable, alone. An obvious target.

Don't let them get to her . . .

And then, suddenly, he caught sight of her in the distance, walking away, a man and a woman on either side of her.

Oh God, I'm too late!

Rachel was shivering. She didn't know how long

she'd been crouching in the doorway. It offered little protection from the rain, which was still pouring down, and every now and again a gust of wind would blow it in, drenching her.

She was numb. She couldn't think. If Jack wasn't with her, she was lost. She hadn't got much money, the police were looking for her and she didn't know what to do or where to go.

A few people hurried past, their umbrellas up, either not noticing her or glancing quickly at her and then looking away, embarrassed.

She could feel the tension growing in her, building up to an unbearable pitch, the voices starting up again, jumbled, shouting. Somewhere in the muddle she thought she could hear Jack's voice but it was drowned out by the others.

Her fingers were trembling and wet with rain as she fumbled in her bag and took out her razor.

She didn't notice the couple approach. She didn't realise that they'd been watching her ever since she got off the train, had seen her attach herself to the old woman and go to the café with her. They'd waited until she was away from the crowds and followed her at a distance as she ran out of the station. Now, suddenly, they were here, standing over her, leaning in towards her.

The woman was speaking softly to her.

Rachel drew back nervously, flattening her back against the ungiving door behind her.

'Go away! Leave me alone!' But it was a weak protest.

The woman crouched down, holding her umbrella above her head, sheltering herself and Rachel. 'Don't worry, love,' she said. 'We're not the police or the social services.'

Rachel relaxed a fraction. 'Who are you? What do you want?'

The woman stretched out her hand and put it over Rachel's. Rachel noticed her heavily made-up face. She stared up at it and the woman dropped her eyes.

'We can help you, love,' she said. 'We can give you food and somewhere to stay.'

Rachel frowned, suspicious. Why should these strangers help her? What was in it for them?

Sensing the question, the man standing behind the woman spoke up. 'You can do some work for us,' he said lightly. 'We help girls like you.'

Girls like you, echoed in Rachel's head.

Jack, where are you? What shall I do?

But there was no answering voice in her head, just the jumble of other voices and the tune, back again, louder than ever.

The woman tightened her grip on Rachel's hand.

'Come on, love,' she said. 'Let's get you out of this rain.'

As the woman pulled her to her feet, the razor fell

from Rachel's hand and clattered onto the ground. The man picked it up and put it in his pocket.

'That's mine!' said Rachel.

'All right, dear,' he said smoothly. 'I'll give it back when we get to our place.'

Stumbling, her legs cramped from having sat huddled up, Rachel allowed herself to be led away between the two of them.

'RACHEL!' Jack concentrated as hard as he could, trying to speak directly to her voices, make himself heard, but she didn't turn towards him, didn't stop.

He knew the sort they were, that man and that woman. No one needed to spell it out to him. He couldn't bear to think that they'd come this far and she'd end up back where she'd started, back at the place he'd taken her from.

I have to reach her. Somehow I have to get to her.

Then suddenly Jasper pricked up his ears and lifted his head.

He'd seen Rachel. Recognised her.

'Go on, boy,' Jack urged him.

It didn't matter if the dog hadn't heard Jack. He bounded forward, covering the ground easily with his long, loping strides.

The man and woman had hailed a cab and were urging Rachel to get in. Tentatively, she put one leg in through the doorway when the bullet of muscle and fur crashed into her from behind.

'What the –?' began the man.

Rachel twisted round. 'Jasper!' she yelled, jumping back from the cab and leaning down to hug the dog.

Her head cleared for a moment and she heard his voice again.

Don't go with them, Rach. I'm here. I'm with you.

Rachel hesitated and the woman gripped her hand firmly.

'Come on, love, don't be silly,' said the woman. 'We can help you.'

Rachel tried to pull her hand away but she couldn't free it and now the man was pushing her from behind.

'No!' said Rachel, her voice rising. 'Leave me alone. I don't want to go with you.'

But the man pushed harder and Rachel felt her feet leave the ground as he was half lifting her into the cab. The driver looked on curiously.

'Teenagers!' said the woman, shrugging her shoulders at him.

Then suddenly there was a loud growl and a confusion of snarling and cursing, and the man fell back, yelling, holding his arm.

'Bloody animal!'

The woman turned, releasing her grip on Rachel, giving her just enough time to duck under her arm and run, sobbing, slipping on the wet ground, panting with effort. She didn't look round to see if they were following her but headed back towards the station. Moments later, Jasper was loping along beside her until he suddenly slid to a stop close to the station entrance.

Rachel almost collided with him. She leaned over, gasping, and put her hand on his head.

'Is he here?'

Stupid. How can I expect a dog to answer?

Fearfully, she looked behind her. In the distance, up in the street, she saw the man and woman getting into the cab, the man still holding his arm. But she knew she couldn't relax.

Where are you, Jack?

She moved off and stood to one side of the entrance away from all the crowds coming in and out of the station, but Jasper went to the opposite side.

He knows where he is.

She followed Jasper and together they stood in the shadow of a great stone archway. Rachel put out a hand to the dog and he licked it. A few passers-by gave them curious glances but on the whole they were ignored. Rachel pulled her hood further over her face.

They'll be here soon.

Rachel jerked her head up and looked around. It was him. He was here? Of course he was here; how else would Jasper have got here?

Jack?

Then the voice in her head. *I'm here, Rach. But you won't see me again. Listen, there are some people looking for you.*

'Too right. Half the bleeding world's looking for me.'

Shh. That's not what I meant. There are other people here. People who will look after you. People we . . . I know about.

'Huh, you just told me not to go with that couple, didn't you?'

They were sex workers.

'Oh God!'

She swallowed nervously. It had been that close. What would have happened to her?

I can't trust anyone.

Then the voice in her head again.

You can, Rach, believe me. There are good people. There are some here. Look, over by the clock, talking to that boy sitting underneath it.

She screwed up her eyes and stared. 'How do I know they won't try the same thing?'

They'll have ID. They're for real. They come here every day. They'll take you somewhere safe and look after you.

'Who are they?'

The voice in her head was very faint now.

Just trust them, Rach. Trust me. They'll help you.

'No, they won't. They'll hand me over.'

Trust me. She could hardly hear him now.

'Don't leave me, Jack.'

I can't stay.

And then silence. Suddenly Jasper was at her side. Rachel put her hand down and stroked his head and the dog looked up at her.

'He's gone now, boy. It's just you and me.'

Very slowly, Rachel walked down the steps and towards the clock, Jasper at her heels. She dragged her feet, not taking her eyes off the two people squatting down, talking to the boy huddled in a blanket on the ground. A man and a woman again. How did she know they, too, weren't sex workers?

They looked up when she approached.

'I'm homeless,' she said simply. 'And the police are looking for me.'

Who had put the words into her mouth?

The woman stood up slowly. She showed her a plastic card slung round her neck. Rachel stared at it. She couldn't read the word on the card.

'You're not the social are you?' Rachel asked.

The woman shook her head. She began to show the card again but then let it fall. 'No,' she said gently. 'We're not the social. But we can help you.' Then she started to tell Rachel about the hostel they ran, the support they offered, how they could help her get her life back on track.

'I'm scared,' said Rachel. She started to cry then, fiercely wiping away the tears with her sleeve.

The man spoke. 'There's no need to be scared,' he said. 'We'll make sure you're safe.'

Safe. Could she trust them?

The woman put her hand out towards Jasper and he licked it.

'And the dog?' asked Rachel.

'Yes. We'll look after the dog.'

'His name's Jasper.'

At the hostel, they showed her to her bedroom. It was small but it was clean with a cheerful duvet on the bed.

'And you won't dob me in?' It must have been the hundredth time she'd asked it.

'No. We won't dob you in and we won't send you anywhere you don't want to go. We'll help you get back on your feet. That's what we do here.'

When they were showing her round the hostel, they talked about getting her into school and getting her help with her reading. Somehow it came out that she liked singing. They showed her a room where there were some musical instruments including an old guitar. When she picked it up they asked her if she'd like to learn to play it.

She didn't have to pretend here. 'I never learned

much at school,' she blurted out.

'You're young. It's not too late to start again.'

The jumble of voices in her head had cleared and Jack's voice was coming through now.

They can sort you out, Rach. Give them a chance. Please, for my sake, stick it out. You can make something of yourself, believe me.

It was then that she started to cry. No one tried to stop her but someone led her back to her room and sat beside her on the bed, holding her hand.

Later she took out Jack's drawing of the dog, smoothing out the creases. She stared at it for a long time. In a few lines he'd captured Jasper's character, those big, intelligent eyes, the lift of the head, the one wonky ear. The drawing was real, wasn't it? She'd been with him when he'd done it. She pinned it to the wall in her room, then she traced over the fluid lines of pencil with her fingers.

You were brilliant at drawing, Jack.

She stared at it for a long time, squinting at the bold signature on the bottom, knowing now what it said.

You'll never be able to do what you wanted, will you? But you can, Rach.

She sniffed and then drew her hand across her nose. As she did so, her sleeve rode up her arm and she saw the dried blood on the new raw cut.

Stay with me, Jack.

In your head. Sometimes. When I can.

Jack

before

Running, no idea where. Running away from the smell of beery breath, the vice-like grip, trembling, sobbing with shame, and ending up slumped in the doorway of a shop to sleep. I'd made no friends in the new place; I had nowhere to go.

An hour later my phone rang. Mum. I couldn't answer it. She'd never forgive me.

Just hearing her voice would make me want to cry.

I switched off my phone. That was the first night I'd spent sleeping rough. I moved away then, away from the town I hated so much, always on the run, knowing that I'd be on the missing persons list, knowing I was wanted by the police.

I got mugged almost straight away. They took my phone and the little money I had too. And then I got ill, not daring to go to see a doctor. Then, that dreadful night when I stumbled and knocked my head and lay bleeding in the road, too weak to move.

I didn't want to die. The car that hit me stopped immediately, the driver horrified. The man got out and knelt over me, phoning emergency services. I saw it happen – an out of body experience. I looked down on my own broken body lying in the road.

Chapter 13

The first weeks at the hostel were hard. Rachel had always had a problem with authority but Jack was right: it was different here. Here they talked about her future as if she had one, as if she was worth something. And they sorted stuff for her.

There were times when she kicked off, of course, but they handled it, were used to it. And they listened. It took weeks but slowly, haltingly, she told them about Adam. Told them what she knew, the evidence that would finally convict him of an even greater crime, and was reassured, over and over, that she wouldn't be named in his trial, that she could remain anonymous.

She told them about the drugs and the cutting, too, and about not being able to read much, about wanting to sing. And no one put her down.

They even let Jasper stay with her and one of the

staff taught her how to feed him properly and took them both to the park every day so he could get some exercise. And at night he lay in her room, beside her bed.

She never told anyone about the voices. That was a secret she had only ever shared with Jack. She still heard them but mostly they were not so loud and horrible, only interfering with her head when she was really stressed or upset. And the other voice, the calm voice, came more often, with the tune – that tune she knew would never go away until she made it her own.

And sometimes, very occasionally, she thought she heard Jack, encouraging her, urging her on when she was giving up, sometimes even laughing at her.

It was Jack who kept her going, the memory of him, the echo of his voice in her head.

There were kids she met in the hostel who'd had an even worse time than her and slowly she let herself reach out to people, make friends without the certainty of rejection. She was terrified of going back to school but when she got there, she wasn't as bad as she'd thought. She had help, a woman chosen for her by the hostel, and once she forgot to be scared, she began to make progress.

At the hostel she spent most of her time in the music room. Voluntary music teachers came in, other kids became interested and they formed a band.

Gradually, as her confidence grew, Rachel started to write songs for the band. She was the only one who wanted to sing the solos, though, and when she sang, it was as if the world went away. The bad things in her life receded and the song took over. And when she sang in a crowded room, she could hold an audience in the palm of her hand.

She had been at the hostel for three months before she plucked up the courage to do it. By this time she had a phone – just a cheap one given to her by a staff member who was upgrading. One evening, alone in her room, she took the grimy, much creased piece of lined paper from her bag and smoothed it out carefully.

She won't be there, she thought. *She'll be long gone.*

She waited, her palms sweaty, as the phone rang and rang.

She wouldn't leave a message. What could she say after all this time? Then, just as the answerphone was about to kick in, the phone was picked up.

Tracey's voice.

Rachel couldn't speak. She held the phone to her ear trying not to cry.

'Who is this? If you're some heavy breathing perve, get off my phone!'

And then, through her tears, Rachel began to

laugh. 'Trace,' she said, hiccuping, 'it's Rach.'

For a moment there was silence, then, so loud that Rachel nearly dropped the phone: 'OH MY GOD! WHAT TOOK YOU SO LONG!'

The pull was overwhelmingly strong, but Jack fought against it.

Give me a little longer.

Distance was no problem to him now and he travelled unencumbered, ethereal.

Mum was in her studio. She was humming as she worked, looking relaxed, happy even, and on the windowsill there was a big pottery vase full of wild flowers. Through the window he could see the twins chasing each other around the garden, laughing and shouting, their voices mingling with the screech of seagulls.

It was as if Kevin had never existed. They were back where they belonged, in the village they'd left.

He stood there, watching her, taking in for the last time how she looked: small and dark haired, frowning slightly as she always did when she was concentrating. It was obvious from her body language that she was no longer tense and frightened but confident and content as she leaned back, squinting critically at the painting on the easel.

He knew she couldn't see him but, as he stared

at her, absorbing every feature, she suddenly turned round and stood quite still, her expression puzzled.

Had she sensed his presence?

She put down her brush and smoothed back a loose strand of hair with her hand, tucking it behind her ear.

An unbearably familiar gesture.

Then she reached for a photo on the bookcase – a photo of him and Dad standing on top of a hill together, laughing, wind-blown, Dad's arm around his shoulders.

She looked at it and smiled, tracing the outline of their faces with her finger, then she held it tightly to her chest for a moment before putting it back.

And he knew then, for certain, that she had forgiven him.

If he could have, he would have shouted out loud with relief, for in that moment he understood, finally, why he'd been sent back so often.

He'd thought it was to atone for his crime.

But it wasn't that. He didn't need to: he'd been forgiven long ago. He had acted in self-defence and no one else had blamed him – not Mum, not anyone. He could see that now.

It was so simple. If he wanted to move on, then all he needed to do was to forgive *himself*.

That was why Rachel had been his final mark.

Sticking with her, finding that spark of talent within

her, learning to respect it, encourage it, knowing that he was helping her, had begun the process of dislodging the huge burden of guilt he'd been carrying ever since he'd killed Kevin.

And now, at last, it was gone and he was released.

He watched his mum for a little longer, then, as the pull became irresistible, he gave into it, not with resentment but with joy and anticipation.

Ten Years Later

A young woman with long, sleek brown hair is sitting in a television studio, her guitar slung across her chest and her knees pressed tightly together. Her eyes are wary as she looks at the man sitting across from her but she keeps still. She knows, now, how bad it looks when you fiddle with your hair or chew your nails. She also knows the sort of questions she will be asked.

The interviewer starts. 'Your first hit single, Rachel – how does it feel?'

He is youngish but with that air of confidence that still has the effect of undermining her, making her feel off balance.

'Yeah, it's great. I'm really pleased.'

He asks a few more questions – and then the one she dreads.

'You've come a long way, Rachel.'

She sighs, quietly. 'How do you mean?' She knows

where this is leading. Why can't they ever let it go?

'Well, you grew up in care, didn't you? Had quite a troubled childhood as I understand it.'

She presses her knees more tightly together. 'That has nothing to do with the person I am now.' She pauses. 'And it has nothing to do with my new single either.' She raises her head and looks the young man full in the eye. She notices the beginning of a flush on his cheeks.

'No, no, of course not, but I just thought the listeners –'

'And I thought we were here to talk about my new single.'

He is definitely blushing now and stutters over his next question.

'Y-yes. Of course we are. It's a most unusual tune – where did it come from?'

'It's a tune I've had in my head for a very long time, but I could never find the lyrics to go with it, to do it justice.'

I know what you're doing, Jack. You're putting posh words into my mouth. Go away!

'And now you have?'

She smiled. 'I hope so.'

'Just one more question, Rachel. The dedication – *for Jack*. Can I ask who Jack is?'

A long silence. Then: 'No, it's private.'

The interviewer smiles nervously. 'Fair enough.' He turns to the studio audience. 'Ladies and gentlemen, Rachel will now sing us her new hit single, the remarkable "Guardian Angel".'

The young woman rises from her chair to thunderous applause and walks slowly over to the mike. When she reaches it, she stops and looks out into the audience, searching for a particular face.

There it is. Her best friend, Tracey. Sitting in the front row on the edge of her seat, grinning fit to burst, giving her a thumbs up and mouthing, 'Good luck!'

The young woman smiles back, then drops her gaze and puts her fingers in place for the first chord.

She waits until there is complete silence, and then she begins.

About the Author

ROSEMARY HAYES has written over forty books for children, several of them shortlisted for awards, including the Kathleen Fidler Award for her first book, *Race Against Time*. Rosemary has worked in publishing and, as well as writing stories, she runs creative writing workshops and is a reader for an authors' advisory service.

She lives in a farmhouse in rural Cambridgeshire.

You can visit her website www.rosemaryhayes.co.uk

Discover more stories

you'll love

at

troikabooks.com

 #troikabooks

troika books